THE LOVE SERIES

Volume One

FIONA DAVENPORT

Copyright © 2019 by Fiona Davenport

Cover designed by Elle Christensen

Edited by Manda Lee

All rights reserved.

No part of this book may be reproduced in any form or by any electronic or mechanical means, including information storage and retrieval systems, without written permission from the author, except for the use of brief quotations in a book review.

 Created with Vellum

The Love Series
VOLUME ONE

3 billionaire romances.
6 brand-new epilogues.
Lots of babies.
All the love.

His Love: Justice will give Blair more than just his love.

Her Love: All Thatcher needs is Imogene's love.

Their Love: Nothing is as important as Jamison & Hazel's love.

His Love

Billionaire Justice Kendall thought he was content with his life. Right up until the day he noticed that his neighbor's daughter had become the beautiful woman who was meant to be his. Since then, he waited not-so patiently for her to turn eighteen.

He bided his time by watching over her. When he realized that all she wanted was a baby of her own, he was ready to give her more than just his love.

He'd give her everything.

Chapter 1
JUSTICE

"Blair." I nodded to the young girl shuffling up to the elevator in her school uniform. Her long blonde hair was pulled away from her face in a high ponytail, giving her no way to hide the pink blush that bloomed on the apples of her cheeks. She glanced up shyly with her big, blue eyes and bit her plump bottom lip.

Fuck. I had to clench my hand into a fist so that I didn't tug her lip from between her teeth and bite it myself. Her sweet looks always tested my control around her. It didn't help that she was practically the poster girl for a naughty school-girl costume. Her shyness only added to the innocent picture and completed the vision of every man's wet dream.

Despite being only seventeen, Blair Gleason had the body of a woman. I'd barely noticed my neighbor's daughter over the years until one day when she was sixteen, we'd bumped into each other at the elevator, just like today—just like we do every day now. I'd greeted her without giving her much attention, but then she'd dropped her backpack and everything had spilled out around her feet. She'd spun around and bent over, giving me a perfect view of her lush, round ass in plain, white cotton panties.

I was instantly hard as a fucking rock and couldn't keep my eyes from drifting down her shapely legs. Even with all her curves, she was still a tiny thing. She was at least a foot shorter than my six-foot-five height, which meant I towered over her. With my muscular frame, I practically dwarfed her, but I immediately knew we would fit together perfectly. Blinking rapidly and taking a few deep breaths, I scolded myself for lusting after a child. I was only a few years shy of being twenty fucking years older than her. The silver streaks at my temples and peppered throughout my goatee were a reminder of that whenever I looked in the mirror. I held in a frustrated groan and hurried to help her pick up her things. But when she straightened and slung her bag over her shoulder again, it thrust out her chest and made it impossible not to notice her big tits and how they bounced when she shifted from foot to foot.

My eyes swept over her from head to toe, taking in the sight of the woman she'd turned into all of a sudden. She'd lost the softness of her baby face, but her lips were still bee-stung and puffy. Lips that New York high society women spent thousands of dollars trying to achieve with collagen. Lips that would make a porn star jealous because they would look so fucking perfect wrapped around a cock. Her neck and shoulders were slender, her waist small, but the swell of her hips made it clear that she was made for breeding.

To my complete shock, my cock had started leaking come at the thought of being the one to fill her belly. It was the first day of my living hell. I hadn't realized it at the time, but the next two years were going to be my purgatory. It was no less than I deserved for thinking about sinking into her teenage pussy and filling her ripe womb with my seed.

"Hello, Mr. Kendall," she whispered in a return greeting, drawing me out of my reverie. Whenever she blushed and peeked at me through her lashes like that, she made me think of a cute little bunny.

I smiled gently and gave in to the urge to brush my finger lightly over her jaw. "Justice," I scolded her teasingly. "How many times do I have to tell you to call me Justice?" It was just another form of torture. Hearing my name fall from her lips in her musical voice only made me that much more desperate to hear her screaming it while I was eleven inches deep.

"Sorry," she blushed even deeper and smiled sweetly at me, her hands clutching the strap of her bag tightly. "Good morning, Justice."

"How is school?"

Blair shrugged. "I'm glad I'll be graduating this year."

The elevator dinged, and the door slid open. We stepped into the car, and I pressed the button for the lobby before responding. "And what are your plans after graduation?" I infused my tone with curiosity, hiding the fact that I didn't care what she had planned. I already knew what she'd be doing when she graduated, and she'd know soon enough too.

"I don't know." She shrugged and looked up at me through her long, pale lashes. "Daddy wants me to go to one of the Ivy League schools I've been accepted into."

I raised a brow and shoved my hands in my pockets to keep from touching her. "And that's not what you want?" I had to keep the bite out of my voice at the thought of her going away to college.

Blair shook her head. "I've never really wanted to go to college, but I want to work with kids, so I'll probably focus on getting my degree in early childhood development. I've already got a jump start on it since I'm in a program that substitutes some of my high-school classes for college courses"—she ducked her head and shrugged—"My dad won't be happy about it, but I think I'll keep attending Hunter College."

I almost showed my relief by expelling a deep breath. It was good to know I didn't have a fight on my hands about that. If Blair wanted to finish her degree, I would support her completely. But she'd be doing it locally, at a school in New York City, while I kept her busy having my babies. I'd be happy to quiz her on her homework while she bounced on my dick.

Son of a bitch. I shook away the images before I came in my pants like a horny teenager and scared the fuck out of my girl. I mentally shook my head at myself. It was a year later, and I still had no control over my thoughts around her.

Only one more year. Only one more year. I chanted to myself. It wasn't even a full year. Just until the end of May, right before graduation. I could be patient.

"I'm excited about an internship I have for the school year, though!" I refocused on Blair, hoping to be distracted from my depraved thoughts. Her tone had become animated, and her beautiful face lit up like the Fourth of July. "I guess they had a spot open up in the in-house daycare at K-Corp. Someone reached out to one of my professors, and she recommended me! They are even allowing me to use it as a practicum for one of my classes. I just hope I don't disappoint them."

I already knew about her internship. I'd been the one to facilitate it. Ever since I started paying attention to her, I noticed and heard everything she said, even the silent thoughts she conveyed so clearly on her face. Blair wore her every emotion, and for some reason she was particularly easy for me to read. Though, she clearly didn't realize how attuned to her I was, or she'd know I'd heard her when she mentioned her love of kids, the college courses she was taking, and all the other details of her life that I clung to as though they were water and I was dying of thirst.

The elevator reached the lobby, and I silently cursed since it meant my time with Blair was over for the day. For the most part.

I gestured for her to walk off first, then kept in step with her as we exited the building into the crisp October air. Before she could turn in the opposite direction as me, I put my hand on her shoulder and waited for her to meet my gaze.

I smiled softly and winked at her. "I'm sure you're perfect for the job." Blair's face flushed with red at my compliment, but she smiled brightly.

"Thanks, Mr—Justice." Then she spun around and trotted to the corner of Central Park West and disappeared around it, heading towards her Upper West Side private school. A soft wind blew, and it ruffled her sorry excuse for a skirt. I needed to do something about that. The thought of some horny teenage boy seeing what was mine had me on the verge of a homicidal rage. I took several deep breaths until I'd calmed down.

"See you later, bunny," I murmured before stalking over to my town car that had been idling a few feet away. I waved off Benjamin, my driver, when he began to exit the vehicle and opened my own door, then slid onto the back seat. He also served as my bodyguard, a necessary evil when you were worth more than a billion dollars.

With the tinted windows and dark interior, the ambiance matched my mood. I put the partition up so that I was alone and unzipped my pants, releasing my turgid cock. I placed a towel underneath my erection before laying my head back against the supple leather. I curled my hands around the edge of the seat and clenched them, holding on like I was afraid I'd be swept away in a tide. Then, like every day on the drive to Wall Street, I closed my eyes and allowed myself to indulge in my morning fantasy.

Chapter 2
JUSTICE

I caressed Blair's swollen belly as I kissed my way down to her naked pussy. I loathed the idea of anything between us, so I demanded that she keep it bare for me. There was nothing sexier than seeing her southern lips glistening with a mixture of her arousal and my seed.

My mouth watered as I leaned in and inhaled deeply, filling my lungs with the sweet and musky scent of her sex. I was addicted to eating her pussy, but for some reason, when she was pregnant, my obsession intensified and I craved it with a deep, gnawing hunger.

With one lick up her seam, Blair was already squirming and whimpering for release. I sucked lightly on her clit before dragging my tongue through her wetness again.

"Please, Justice," she begged. "I want you inside me."

I grinned against her pussy. My girl loved my cock and I

was more than happy to oblige her, but I needed my taste first. "Patience, bunny," I crooned. Then I buried my face in her heat and licked and sucked, eating her and drinking down all her juices.

When she was pumping her hips up to meet my mouth and crying out my name, I latched onto her clit and plunged two fingers into her channel. With one swipe over her most sensitive spot, she came with a scream and a flood of her arousal filled my mouth.

"Fuck," I mumbled as I continued to lap at her and lazily pump my fingers. "I love it when you squirt your come down my throat."

I was pressing my pelvis hard into the mattress to try and relieve some of the pressure and keep from coming before I was balls-deep in her young pussy. Blair had learned to take me all the way like a champ. After one baby, you'd think she would loosen up, but she was still as tight and innocent as the day I popped her cherry. Just thinking about it made me want to roar like a fucking caveman.

I surged up between her legs, staying upright on my knees so I wasn't leaning over and putting pressure on her round belly. Grabbing her ass, I elevated her so that I had the perfect angle to thrust in to the hilt. From this position, I had the perfect view of my cock disappearing into her pussy with the proof that I'd bred her right above.

The slight abrasions on her thighs from my whiskers and

the sight of my cock coming out sticky and shiny from her come was enough to set me off right then. However, I managed to keep from completely blowing my load, though I was leaking a steady stream of come. "I swear you've gotten even tighter since I knocked you up, bunny," I grunted as I fought to draw my dick out of her so I could shove it back in. "You're squeezing the fuck out of my cock. Oh, fuck. Yes!"

I started slow, trying to draw it out. But as usual, once I got inside her, my body took over. "I can't hold back, baby," I gritted through clenched teeth. "I need you to come." Her pussy walls started to flutter then clench as shudders wracked her body. "Such a good girl," I praised, pressing on her clit to push her over the edge.

Blair began to chant, "Yes, yes, yes." Then she screamed as her orgasm crashed over her. "Justice!"

"Fuck!" I shouted. "Oh yeah, baby. Take it. Fuck, yes!" Black spots filled my vision as I came with a vengeance, like being hit by a fucking freight train. Thick, strong jets of jizz spurted from my dick, filling her womb. I'd just had her a few hours ago to take care of my morning wood, but it seemed as though I had an endless supply of cream.

Eventually, my eyes cleared, and my erratic breathing slowed. I pulled out and grinned when Blair mewled in protest. "You still hungry for my cock, bunny?"

Her porn star lips turned down in an adorable pout, and she nodded. She looked so fucking beautiful with her long blonde hair wildly around her, her flushed skin, and her passion filled, blue eyes. My gaze drifted down to her large, milky tits. She was still nursing our first baby and drops of white liquid were beading on her nipples before dripping down the sides. She'd had a fantastic set before she got pregnant, but once she was knocked up, they'd grown to accommodate her supply of milk. I was almost as addicted to them as I was to her pussy.

Who was I kidding? I was obsessed with every part of Blair.

"Daddy needs his turn with your tits first," I told her; then I licked my lips in anticipation. Her arms had been spread out beside her, gripping the sheets, but she moved them to her belly as she watched me with a heavy-lidded gaze. My cock had barely softened, and it immediately swelled to epic proportions when Blair slid her palms up to cup the heavy globes. She squeezed gently, causing more of her nectar to spill from the ripe mounds.

I growled and quickly—carefully—rolled onto my back and put her astride me. She dropped down hard and fast, crying out when my tip hit her cervix. Grasping her hips, I sat up and took one succulent nipple into my mouth. I fed from her tits until I was satisfied, and she was riding me like I was a prized stud.

"Gently, bunny," I cautioned, worried about her being too rigorous while she was so far along.

"I can't help it," she panted as she rose up and dropped back down fast and hard.

Taking ahold of her lush, wide hips, I held her still and took over, pounding up into her pussy so I was doing all of the work.

Blair threw her head back and cried out in ecstasy as she splintered apart. I buried myself as deep as possible and latched onto one of her nipples again and bit. Not enough to really hurt, but enough to cause a spark of pain to mix with her pleasure. I knew it would intensify her orgasm, and I was rewarded with a deafening scream that echoed off the walls of our bedroom. Her pussy was wrapped so tightly around my cock that I couldn't have moved it if I wanted to.

I switched to the other nipple, and I detonated when her milk splashed into my mouth. The world ceased to exist as I came with such violence that I briefly wondered if I would survive. Who the fuck cared? I wouldn't want to go any other way.

My eyes popped open as the sound of my shout filled the back of the town car. Thankfully, the partition was soundproof, something I'd corrected after the first time I had my little fantasy.

I released my death grip on the bench seat and glanced down at my lap; grimacing at the sticky mess I'd made. Another lesson I learned after I'd ruined several pairs of pants. I stocked the car with hand towels when I realized I might as well give in to my morning day-dream because I always lost when I tried to fight it.

The crazy thing was, I hadn't even touched myself. Nobody else had either since I hadn't been interested in a woman since long before Blair. And I'd never needed to take myself in hand because my dick didn't have any reason to get hard. Then, once Blair became my obsession, I still didn't have the desire to take care of myself, despite sporting at least a semi pretty much all the time. It felt too much like betrayal. The only one who should be touching me, satisfying me, was my woman. And even in my dreams, she was able to do it.

I quickly cleaned up and threw the towel into a duffle bag I kept in the car for that exact reason. I dropped it at the cleaners on the weekends so that I was prepared again Monday morning.

The car slowed to a stop in front of my building just as I was tucking my somewhat limp dick back into my pants. I zipped up right before Benjamin opened my door. After a cursory glance to make sure no traces of my activities remained, I exited the vehicle.

At least I had my work, which I loved, to help keep my obsession from consuming my every thought throughout the day. Otherwise, I wasn't sure I'd have been able to stay away until the right time. There were so many days when I'd almost said fuck it and gave in to my need for her. But then logic would rear its ugly head and remind me that she'd be eighteen soon. I could wait.

Chapter 3
JUSTICE

"Thatcher's in your office," Patti, my secretary, announced when I reached her desk, situated just outside my door.

I sighed—pretending I didn't already know why he was there—and speared her with a reproachful glare. "What the hell, Patti? What happened to being the gatekeeper?" Patti had been my secretary since my brother and I started our investment firm, K-Corp, fifteen years ago. She was in her early fifties now, had been married for over thirty years, and had three kids who were grown and lived in the city.

She'd been the first person to apply for the job, and my brother and I had instantly fought over who got to hire her as their assistant. Luckily, I won the coin toss. But she'd been more mother to both us than our own ever had been. Her husband and kids were family to us, too.

"Language, young man!" she snapped, pointing her pen at me.

I rolled my eyes since Patti could curse with the best of them. "Sorry, ma'am."

She nodded and patted her short, brown bob, brushing hair out of her face as she turned her attention to her computer screen.

"Um, Patti?"

"Hmmm?"

I put my hands on my hips and scowled. "Thatcher?"

"Oh yes, he's in your office," she repeated distractedly.

"Why?" I pressed.

"Because you're a selfish son-of-a-bitch and I have a fucking bone to pick with you." My brother stepped out of my office as he spoke, clearly fuming about something. Again, I pretended not to know why and simply raised a questioning brow.

"What he said," Patti added with a grin. Shit, she obviously knew why Thatcher was there too.

"Et tu, Patti?"

She just shrugged and started typing.

"I'm surrounded by crazy people," I grumbled with a shake of my head as I brushed past Thatcher into my office. "Enlighten me," I said to him as I took a seat at my glass desk, my back to the spectacular view of the Upper Bay and the Statue of Liberty.

"You seriously didn't expect me to put up a fight when you foisted the Benson account on me?"

"Mr. Benson is one of our biggest clients, Thatch"—I leaned back in my chair and looked him straight in the eye—"He needs the best of the best, and that's you."

Thatcher's gray eyes, so much like my own, narrowed. "Don't bullshit me, bro. You just don't want to deal with his vapid wife."

I shrugged and picked up a silver pen from the desktop to fiddle with. "Maybe it's both."

"She's already sent me five texts this morning, called twice, and emailed about setting up a 'private' appointment." He walked to my desk and bent over so our faces were level. "I get why you did it. I know you don't want her showing up in the lobby and causing drama while Blair is in the building." I glanced at the open door to my office, then back to Thatcher frowning in warning. My brother and I were only a year apart and had always been close. We were best friends, and he was the only one who knew about my obsession with Blair. I wanted to keep it that way. He nodded in acknowledgment and lowered his voice. "But, pawning that succubus off on me?" Thatcher furrowed his brow and scowled. "You owe me big time, bro."

"I do," I agreed. My immediate capitulation seemed to un-bunch his panties, and the tension left his body.

He slumped down into one of the chairs across from me and put his feet up on my desk. "She starts today?"

I nodded, attempting to appear calm and unruffled, but the pen tapping a fast rhythm on the glass betrayed my agitated state.

Thatcher dropped his feet and sat forward, resting his elbows on his knees and steepling his fingers. His expression was dead serious. "You have to stay away," he said quietly.

Irrational anger streaked through me, but I managed to keep a damper on it. I opened the center drawer and tossed the pen inside with more force than was necessary. "I know."

———

UNABLE TO RESIST ANOTHER MINUTE, I picked up my phone and swiped to open it. Then I found the app I was looking for and loaded it.

The daycare had several mounted cameras that allowed me to keep an eye on Blair while she was there. But, I'd worked out a curriculum with the instructor for her practicum that also required her to use a new app that was becoming standard in the industry. It was a real-time app that allowed the teachers to have instant access to medical history and other notes, as well as reminders and notifications from the parents. Parents could receive screenshots and video throughout the day, even using the app to request a photo or video update.

Blair had been given a phone—one I'd provided that allowed me to keep track of her location. Theoretically, so that I would worry less about her safety. However, while it helped a little, I knew I wouldn't be satisfied until I was personally seeing to her safety.

The app was another tool to help me keep from doing something stupid. I'd made sure it came already installed and set up on her phone. Blair was instructed to use it throughout the day to keep a sort of video diary, especially while she was working in the daycare. I was sure she assumed the information was going to her professor, but I was the only one who had access to her app.

I was excited to see that she'd already uploaded a couple of videos, some notes, and screenshots. I went through them over and over until I had them memorized.

When my alarm went off at six, I closed the app and woke up the screen on my computer. After a few clicks, I was staring at the series of camera feeds in the daycare. They closed at six, so the last of the parents would be picking up their children.

Blair was standing by a window cradling a baby boy, no more than six months old, and swaying from side to side. She was cuddling him, once again reminding me of a sweet little bunny. She looked so natural and at ease. The expression on her face was practically blissful. I imagined it was a hint of the way she would look when I made her come.

A woman walked into the room and called to Blair, who turned around and smiled. If it were anyone but me, they might not have noticed that her smile was off. I leaned in and studied her more intently, anxious to know what was upsetting my girl.

The woman took the baby from Blair and kissed him on the head. She smiled and said something to my bunny, then turned and walked towards the exit.

My eyes remained glued to Blair. It was clear that she thought no one was looking because her mask had dropped away. Blair put her arms around herself, and her face was awash with pure longing as she watched the mother leave with her baby.

Soon, bunny. Soon.

Chapter 4
JUSTICE

Thirty days. Thirty fucking days. I repeated this in my head over and over as I watched Blair reluctantly say goodbye to the babies in her care. Every fucking day of the week, I struggled to keep from running down to her and sweeping her away to take that look off her face.

I only had to endure 30 more days. Then I would be free to take her and give her what she obviously so desperately wanted.

Marriage and kids had never been in my plans until the day Blair became mine. Now, all I could think about was putting the ring burning a hole in my pocket on her finger and filling our penthouse with our little ones.

My eyes stayed glued to the monitors until Blair had slung her purse over her chest and left the daycare. I hated that I couldn't keep watch over her when she wasn't in the building, but I was somewhat appeased by being able to track her phone.

Every day, she would leave after they closed at six and head home to the penthouse next to mine. Whenever possible, I timed it so I would bump into her in our building lobby so we could ride the elevator together. I knew I wasn't strong enough to give her a ride home. If we were alone in the back of my car, I wouldn't be able to withstand her irresistible mix of innocence and sexy and she'd never make it to her eighteenth birthday with her virgin cherry intact.

Instead, I followed her at a distance—something that annoyed Benjamin and made him ridiculously cranky—so that I was sure she was protected. When we were a block away, I flagged down my driver and we pulled up to the building just as she arrived.

Yeah, I was well aware of how fucking crazy I seemed. I could only imagine the field day a shrink would have with this level of obsession, but I honestly couldn't manage to muster up even one fuck to give.

Today was one of the rare days when I wasn't able to personally make sure she got home safely, and it made me grumpy as fuck. I sent Benjamin, who also happened to be former Italian Special

Forces, to trail her and make sure she got home without incident. If he wondered at my odd actions concerning Blair, he never voiced it and I didn't offer an explanation.

Thatcher sauntered into my office, drawing my attention away from the app where I was staring at the little green dot representing my girl.

"Remind me why this meeting had to happen tonight?" I scowled.

"Jamison is getting married this weekend, and he'll be gone on his honeymoon for three months." Thatcher leaned against the doorway; his hands stuffed in his pockets. "We need this merger to go through before the fiscal year ends."

"Okay," I dragged out the word. "But why a dinner meeting? This couldn't have been done during lunch?"

Thatcher's gaze was on the wall of windows that made up the left side of my office, matching the one I sat in front of. He meandered over to look down the forty-five floors to the ground beneath us. "I'm not available for lunch meetings," he finally responded, his tone inattentive.

I stood and walked up beside him, staring in the same direction, trying to discern what he was staring at. The Statue of Liberty? Battery Park, maybe? "Want to give me a little more explanation than that, brother?"

Thatcher cursed and turned away from the window. "She's there. Every day. It's the only time I have to see her."

My brow shot up, probably getting lost in my hairline. This was the first I was hearing of a "she."

"The one," he clarified before turning his dark, churning eyes on me.

I'd never known Thatcher to be anything less than completely confident. Seeing him unraveling at the seams told me how serious he was about this woman. "So, what's the problem? Why are you hesitating?"

He shook his head and pulled his hands from his pockets to cross his arms over his chest. "I'm not hesitating," he disagreed. "I'm just not ready yet. Everything has to be perfect."

"Everything?" I asked, still confused. Why hadn't he just gone and gotten his girl? "What are you waiting for?" The second Blair was legal, I was going to have her moved into our home and installed in our bed with her legs wide open so I could fuck my baby into her unprotected womb. And, I wouldn't let her leave until she'd made me a daddy. Possibly not even then…

Thatcher shook his head. "I'll explain another

time. We're going to be late."

I decided to allow him to table the subject for now, but I'd be getting to the bottom of it later. I returned to my desk and grabbed my suit coat from the back of my chair, donning it. I gathered a stack of files for Patti and set them on her empty desk as we passed by. She'd gone home early for her daughter's birthday dinner. Another event I was missing due to this stupid meeting. Not that I would have gone. I knew I'd been a son-of-a-bitch lately and wasn't fit company.

I was surprised that Benjamin wasn't back yet, but I figured Blair must have stopped at the store on the way home. She cooked for her and her dad most nights. It was something she'd mentioned that she loved to do. Since my driver wasn't available, we grabbed a cab to the midtown steakhouse. I did my best to pay attention to the topic at hand and participate in the conversation, but I kept glancing at my phone, waiting for a text from Benjamin telling me that Blair was home.

Finally, at around eight, I excused myself and made my way outside. The phone only rang once before he picked up.

"What the fuck, B?" I nearly shouted.

"Calm down, Justice. She just got home. I'm headed in your direction."

"What was the holdup? It wouldn't have taken her this long just to go to the store."

"She went to a doctor's office in a building on Park before going to the store."

My whole body stiffened, and my heart leapt into my throat. "Doctor?" I croaked. Was something wrong with my girl?

"I don't think it's something to worry over," he assured me. "The only names listed on the directory were Gynecologists."

I let out the breath I hadn't realized I been holding. It was probably just her yearly checkup. Except…I frowned as I did the math in my head. No, she wasn't due for another three months.

"She did come out with a piece of paper clutched in her hand, though. And when she left the store, she had a pharmacy bag."

My eyes narrowed as his words sunk in, and the most likely scenario formed in my mind. A birth control prescription?

Over my dead fucking body.

"Get your ass here and get me home fast," I growled before hanging up. I shot a text to Thatcher, telling him I had an emergency and he could handle the meeting on his own. We had complete trust in each other, so I wasn't at all worried about leaving it in his hands.

Benjamin rolled to a stop in front of the restaurant and double parked so he could get out and open my door, using it as an excuse to do a visual sweep of the area. He shot me a frown, conveying his displeasure at my choice to dispatch him elsewhere and leave me unprotected.

He was in for a big surprise in a month when he found himself permanently on Blair's detail. Initially, I'd only intended to hire a bodyguard temporarily after some serious threats had been made towards Thatcher and myself while we were in the midst of a huge international deal. But, Benjamin and I had become friends and when I realized the role Blair was going to have in my life, I kept him on, knowing he would eventually be assigned to her. Though, I hadn't shared that plan with him yet.

I climbed into the car and lowered the partition as he got settled into the driver's seat. "I don't care what you have to do," I seethed. "Who you have to bribe, what the fuck ever. Make sure that doctor and all the others in her office refuse to write Blair another prescription."

Again, if Benjamin had questions about my demands, he kept them to himself. He simply nodded and tapped the screen in the dash to search his contacts. I rolled down the window next to me and stopped paying attention. I was lost in thought as I stared out into the dark night and enjoyed the spring breeze. I focused on the goal of getting rid of the birth control because if I thought about who she'd gone on it for, there was a good chance I would lose my mind.

I honestly had no idea what I was going to do when I got home, but I wouldn't rest until I was sure that Blair's body remained ripe and ready for me to breed.

As luck would have it, maybe it was a reward for my patience, Blair would be ovulating when she turned eighteen. I knew because in my fanatical need to know everything about her, I paid close attention. The day her backpack had spilled, a small side pocket had been partially unzipped and a few tampons had fallen out. From that day on, my eyes strayed to the pocket every morning, and I noticed that it was only full once a month.

"Taken care of, Justice." Benjamin's voice pulled me from my thoughts, and I lifted my chin in acknowledgment when he glanced at me in the rearview mirror.

My building came into view, and I was out the door before the car had come to a complete stop. I raced inside and used my fob to unlock the penthouse elevator. I swore a blue streak at the slow ascent and vowed to call the maintenance company and order them to speed it up.

At long last, the car reached the top floor, and the doors whooshed open. My long stride ate up the distance to the door at the opposite end of the hall from mine, but I hesitated when I finally reached it.

The smell of something heavenly was seeping under the door and filling the hallway. My stomach growled, and I pictured the day when I would come home to smells like this coming from my own apartment. And the sight of my barefoot and pregnant wife in the kitchen. Which wouldn't happen as fast as I wanted if I didn't take care of those fucking pills.

I raised my hand and rapped on the door with my knuckles. Heavy footsteps got louder as someone approached the door. Probably Paul, Blair's father, since my girl walked with a light, graceful step. If I didn't know better, I would have thought she floated everywhere, like the angel she was.

After a few more steps, the lock disengaged, and the door swung open. However, it wasn't Paul greeting me from inside the apartment. It was a boy, a teenage punk in a school uniform with the same insignia as Blair's.

Chapter 5
JUSTICE

The little fucker had a cocky smirk on his pretty boy face, but it fell away the minute he clocked my expression. I imagined it looked as deadly as I felt.

"Uh, can I help you?" he stammered, though he tried to sound confident.

I ignored him and pushed inside. "Blair?" I called. Her apartment almost mirrored mine—though mine had a second floor—so I easily navigated straight to the kitchen. I almost fell to my knees at the vision in front of me. Blair's white-blonde hair was piled on top of her head, and she was wearing a white T-shirt and jean shorts that went to just above her knees. Thank fuck, I didn't think I could have handled anything else without my head exploding. She had on a frilly pink apron and her feet were bare, showing off her cute, pink-tipped toes.

Something bubbled on the stove, and she stirred it until I rasped her name again. She jumped, clearly noticing me for the first time. Her cheeks bloomed with that pretty blush I loved so much.

"Where's your dad?" My tone was harsher than I meant for it to be from trying to control myself, and she took a step back. *Fuck fuck fuck.* I hated that I scared her. When I spoke again, I adopted a softer tone. "Is your dad here, bunny?"

I hadn't meant to let the nickname slip, but I enjoyed the slight widening of her eyes and the way the flush of her skin spread.

"He's in his office," she answered quietly.

I turned around and trained my gaze on the little shithead hovering behind me. "Leave." My tone brooked no argument, but the kid clearly had a death wish.

He puffed up his scrawny chest and gave me what I was sure was supposed to be a defiant glare, but just made him look like a pouting toddler. "Blair and I are working on a project."

"Out," I snapped.

He began to protest again but when I took a few menacing steps in his direction, backing him up into the living room, his mouth opened and closed like a fish. Then he caved and yelled, "I need to get going, Blair. We can work at my house next time."

I closed my eyes and pinched the bridge of my nose, willing myself to stay calm. I needed to remember that I couldn't take care of Blair from prison.

I stayed in that position until the front door clicked shut.

"Justice," I heard Blair snap from behind me. I spun around and almost smiled at how adorable she was. Her hands were on her hips, her face was scrunched in indignation, and her blue eyes were lit with fire. My bunny had more mettle than I thought. Why did that make me want her even more? "Our project is a huge portion of my grade, and I have a hard enough time getting him to work on it when we're together."

My eyes narrowed, and my hands clenched into fists. "What are you doing when you're supposed to be working?" Her answer was bound to piss me the fuck off, but I had to know.

Blair blushed and dug the toes of one foot into the thick carpet. "He mostly tries to convince me to go out with him," she sighed.

At that moment, I was more grateful than ever that Blair was an open book to me. She was trying not to be negative, but I could see the annoyance in the downturn of her mouth.

"So, the birth control pills aren't for him?" I blurted. *Well shit. Nice going Justice.*

Blair's eyes became so big they almost swallowed her face, and she blushed so hard her skin was practically tomato red. "How did you…?"

"Answer the question," I cut her off; needing an answer.

Her eyes darted away, and she bit her bottom lip as she fidgeted, twisting her fingers around each other. "No."

"Who?" I prompted sternly.

"Nobody, I mean it was just in case…"

My gaze bored into hers, and she looked back at me with uncertainty. "In case?" I queried.

"I'm going to be eighteen at the end of the month," she explained hesitantly. "I thought maybe…" She was studying my face intently and for the first time, I couldn't discern what she was thinking from her expression or stance. It was unsettling, and I hated it. "Never mind," she said, her shoulders slumping.

Before I could say anything else, Paul strode into the room. "What's for dinner, sweet pea?" He stopped when he saw me and regarded me with confusion. "Justice. Did we have an appointment?"

Paul was a great guy, but he was the epitome of the absent-minded professor. He was the dean over the school of music at The Juilliard School, but he came from family money, which was how he and Blair lived like they did. Despite his wealthy upbringing, he freely admitted that he had no clue how to manage his inheritance. I'd been handling his investments, working alongside his money manager, since I bought the building and moved into the penthouse across the hall. I didn't deal with smaller accounts anymore with only a few exceptions, Paul being one of them. I did it as much for Blair as my friendship with her father.

"No, Paul. I just needed to have a word with Blair. I wanted to offer my car and driver to get her from school to her internship and home."

Blair frowned but didn't have a chance to say anything before Paul smiled widely and nodded emphatically. "That's a generous offer, Justice. Normally, I wouldn't take you up on something bound to inconvenience you, but I do worry about my sweet pea coming home all the way from Wall Street in the evenings."

Blair rolled her eyes. "I've been getting around this city by myself since I was ten, Daddy. I don't think—" I cut her a warning look, and she shut her mouth.

"Still, can't be too careful." Paul walked over to Blair and wrapped his arm around her shoulder, then kissed her temple. After a moment, his eyes shifted back in my direction. "You're welcome to stay for dinner."

"I'm sure he's far too busy," Blair interjected. My stomach chose that moment to emit another hungry rumble.

Paul laughed uproariously and beckoned me in their direction before turning towards the dining room. "I'm sure a bachelor like you rarely has a home cooked meal, and my Blair is a whiz in the kitchen. I don't know how I'd survive without her."

I clamped my jaw together to keep from informing him that he would need to solve that mystery by the end of the month or starve.

"I'll set another place," Blair murmured before disappearing into the kitchen.

There was something I had to do before I could relax and enjoy the meal. I glanced at the kitchen; then gave Paul an innocent smile and cocked my head towards the hallway. "I'm just going to use the restroom."

He mirrored the tilt of my lips and waved in the same direction I'd indicated. "I'm sure you know where it is," he laughed. I nodded and spun on my heel, marching down the hall with purpose. The apartment had three bedrooms, and I guessed right when I pushed open the door to the first one on the right.

The room was decorated in white and lavender with yellow accents; it was feminine without being overkill. Everything was in its place except the stack of worn paperbacks on the nightstand that had me chuckling. Blair had always been a bookworm. It was one of the few things I remembered about her as a child and something we had in common. A grin sliced across my face when I pictured her reaction to one of the improvements I'd made to my home when I moved in.

I knew I didn't have much time before my bathroom excuse became awkward, so I did a quick sweep of the room and decided that the most likely place was the white-washed, antique vanity on the wall by a door that I knew led to an ensuite bathroom. After a thorough examination of the drawers, I came up empty, so I moved on to the washroom.

Figuring it was the most obvious choice, I opened the mirrored door to the medicine cabinet first. A little, round, blue container caught my attention first, and I took it from the shelf. I opened it to find a packet of white pills and grunted in approval when I didn't find any of them missing. It wasn't like I would have had her stomach pumped or anything, but I was still happy not to have to worry about even one pill.

I started popping them out into my palm, one by one. "Justice! What are you doing?" Blair gasped as she rushed into the bathroom and tried to make a grab for the container. I held it above her head, which was easily done considering our height difference, and finished emptying the packet.

I tossed the container into the trash can and stalked over to the small room that contained the toilet. Glancing in Blair's direction, I made sure she was watching when I lifted the lid and tossed the offending pills in and flushed.

She stood in silent shock and just stared at me as I prowled over to her. When I got into her space, she backed up. But I followed, and soon I had her trapped between me and the wall.

"Why did you do that?" she asked in a raspy tone. Her eyes looked suspiciously watery as they locked with mine, and I wanted nothing more than to kiss her and make it better.

"You don't need them," I stated.

"How would you know?" she snipped. Her attempt to be confident was ruined by the pretty shade of pink suddenly dusting over her cheeks and nose.

I leaned down until our lips were only a whisper apart. "Because I can smell that innocent little cherry from here, bunny."

Her mouth formed a little O, and she sucked in a breath. "Um…well, I was hoping to—um—you know—" she stammered, her blush intensifying as she broke eye contact. "Maybe I don't want to be a virgin anymore," she uttered suddenly, then slapped a hand over her mouth.

Blair's eyelids dropped, and she looked shyly up at me through her lashes. "I guess I was hoping the guy I want would want me too." Her voice was soft as a whisper, and her warm breath bathed my lips, making me crave their touch.

"They don't want *you*," I growled thinking about those pricks who only wanted in her panties and weren't interested in the real her, in treating her like she deserved.

Her expression crumbled, and she shrunk into the wall. "Okay. I guess you're right then. I don't need the birth control. Clearly, I won't be having sex if nobody wants me."

My head reared back in disbelief. What the fuck? Then it hit me, how what I said could be misconstrued. "I meant those boys only want one thing from you, bunny," I explained. "They don't want the real you, all of you." I didn't bother to disguise the longing in my voice. "Besides, those little shits wouldn't know the first thing about pleasuring a woman."

"Do you?" Blair asked softly.

My head dipped, and I closed the distance between our faces again. "Do I what?"

"Know what to do in—um—bed?"

A wicked smile curved my lips, and I traced my lips along her cheek, so light they were barely touching, until I reached her ear. "I know how to please *my* woman."

Blair's breathing picked up, and we were so close that her big tits rubbed against my chest. When I felt her hard nipples, I groaned and dropped my face into the crook of her neck. "Thirty days," I rumbled.

"What?" Blair panted.

I slid my hands to her ass and yanked her forward so she could feel every inch of my hard cock pressing into the heat of her pussy. "Thirty fucking days, bunny."

Her hands grasped my biceps, and she gripped them tightly, her nails digging into my skin through my dress shirt. "What's in thirty days?"

One of the threads holding me together snapped, and I gave in to a desperate urge. I brought my head back in position and pressed my mouth to hers. Electricity zinged straight to my dick and sparks flew. One second before I lost it, I forced myself to pull away rather than following my instincts and deepening the kiss.

"In thirty days. You're mine."

Chapter 6
JUSTICE

May thirty-first was officially my favorite day of the year. It was the day Blair graced this world with her glowing presence. It was the day my bunny turned eighteen. And, it was the day she would officially be mine. Fina-fucking-ly.

"You're quite the contradiction today," Patti chirped as she traipsed into my office.

I raised a brow and leaned back in my chair, the fingers of my left hand playing aimlessly with my silver pen. "Contradiction?"

She nodded and set a stack of folders in front of me. "Sign and return to me," she instructed. Then she took a seat in one of the deep, leather chairs in front of me. "If you didn't have that permanent smile plastered on your face, I'd say you were downright grouchy."

"I'm confused," I admitted with a chuckle.

Patti eyed me for a few moments then relaxed in the chair and crossed one leg over the other. "I'm guessing it's impatience." Her tone was calculating, and her probing stare made me squirm in my seat. "Today's the day, isn't it?"

"Pardon?" I watched her warily, wondering what she thought she knew. She couldn't possibly…right?

"She turns eighteen today?"

I gaped at her in silence.

"When are you boys going to realize that I know everything?" she asked smugly.

I laughed and shook my head because she was absolutely right. I didn't know why I deluded myself into thinking she didn't know what was going on.

There was nothing that would stop me from fulfilling my plans, but Patti's opinion did mean a lot to me. It was why I'd hidden my feelings for Blair from her. I was afraid she would tell me that I was too over the top, that my obsession with Blair was unhealthy. That said, it wouldn't stop me, but her disapproval would sting.

"Yes, today is her birthday," I confirmed.

Patti was quiet for a minute, watching me with an unreadable expression. Then she smirked. "You remind me of Don." Don was her husband, and it was a huge compliment to be compared to the man she adored. "I never told you how we met, or what our courtship was like because I wasn't sure how you boys would take it."

I almost blanched at the tiny bit of nervousness in her tone. But I managed to keep my expression neutral. She was nervous about our approval? My chest warmed at the thought that she wanted our respect as much as we wanted hers.

"You'll have to get Don to tell you his side of the story. I'm sure it's very different from mine," she tittered. "My version is that he came, he saw, he kidnapped."

Well shit. I was hooked. I stopped playing with my pen and leaned on the desk to listen intently.

"Don was an intern at my father's firm. They're both architects. Anyway, he saw me bring my dad lunch one day and according to him, he fell for me right that moment. He asked my dad about me, and my father thought I was too young for Don. I had just barely turned eighteen, and Don was fifteen years older than me. So Dad wouldn't give him any information about me or a way to contact me."

Patti's complexion pinkened as she continued, and I was hanging on her every word. "The next time I showed up with lunch, Don was ready. Apparently, he'd been focused on nothing but me for weeks. He caught me at the elevator and dragged me into an empty office." She cleared her throat and sat up primly in her seat. "We'll skip over that; it was the boring part of the story anyway." Her blush and sly smile said otherwise, but I stayed quiet so she would continue. "Fast forward from there and the next thing I knew, I was in Don's car and we were driving to a house he'd rented on the beach in Connecticut."

Patti held out her hand and admired the diamond and gold wedding set on her hand with a soft smile. "He had me running down the aisle less than a week later. Much to my father's frustration. But, after he saw the way Don loved me, he came around fast."

Her point didn't escape me. "You think Blair's dad will come around?" I asked. It was something else that had bothered me, but since it wouldn't change my decision, I hadn't dwelt on it. Still, I wanted my girl to be happy, and it would be hard if her dad wasn't supportive of our relationship.

Patti stood and leaned across my desk to pinch my cheek. I rolled my eyes but took her hand and kissed the back before she took it back. "Don't tell Don I did that," I hurried to say. I may not have known that whole story, but Don's possessiveness and jealousy when it came to Patti was no secret.

"I know you, Justice. If you didn't love this girl with all that you are, you wouldn't be interested at all." She straightened back up and padded over to the door, then paused and looked back at me. "Just be you and love her with everything you've got. What other people think isn't important. Blair is the only one that matters. If you love her like she deserves, if you put her first, her dad will come around."

She stepped through the door but popped her head back in when I called her name. "Thanks." She smiled brightly and nodded. "Now, go get your girl and stop being such an ass around here. Two years is long enough to deal with your Oscar the Grouch routine."

I laughed heartily as she disappeared then followed her instructions, quickly finishing up with a few emails and signing the documents Patti had given me. I handed them to her as I passed her desk. "Take the rest of the day off," I told her. "Actually, you might as well take next week off. I doubt I'll be here."

Patti chuckled and waved me off. "If I'm not here, this place would fall apart." She wasn't wrong.

"But I might leave a little early every day. Now go," she encouraged with a shooing motion.

I grinned and gave her a smart salute before striding to the elevator and taking it to the first floor where the daycare was located. The wait was finally over.

Chapter 7
JUSTICE

When I walked into the daycare, Pandora, the manager, was sitting at the front desk doing paperwork. She looked up with a warm smile, but it turned puzzled when she saw me. "Um, Mr. Kendall, is there something I can do for you?"

I nodded and lifted my chin in the direction of the classrooms. "I'm here for Blair."

Her mouth turned down in a confused frown. "I don't understand, is there a problem? Because she's been doing a fantastic job. She's a natural with the kids."

That put a smile on my face. Yes, my girl was going to be an amazing mother. "There's no problem," I reassured her. "It's her birthday, and we're going to celebrate."

"Oh, okay." She sounded relieved, and I

cocked my head to the side curiously. "I was worried that you were pulling her internship or something." She smiled sheepishly and shrugged. "Honestly, when you told me to hire her, I was skeptical. But now, I really don't know how we could live without her."

"You're the reason they hired me?" We both turned at the sound of Blair's voice. She was standing at the entrance of one of the classrooms, holding an infant in her arms. My dick practically wept at the sight. "Why would they do that just because you asked them to?" she asked, clearly perplexed.

"Mr. Kendall is the boss, Blair," Pandora said with a chuckle. "When he says jump, we say 'how high?'"

Blair's clear blue eyes turned to study me, and I wanted to smack myself upside the head for being so dumb. I'd forgotten that she didn't know I owned the company she worked for or that I'd created her "internship." This wasn't how I'd envisioned her finding out, but that's where we were.

"I created the position, but you were absolutely qualified for it," I told her, holding my hands out to the sides; palms up.

"K-Corp," she said slowly, putting emphasis on the K. "Justice Kendall." She shook her head and closed her eyes, her cheeks turning pink. "I can't believe I never put that together."

I covered the distance between us in two strides and glided my fingertips over her cheeks, then along her jaw. "I wasn't exactly up front about it," I acknowledged softly.

When her eyes opened again, she peered up at me through her lashes, and a bright smile stretched across her face. "I can't believe you did that for me." Her blush deepened, but she lifted her head fully to meet my gaze. "You remembered that I wanted to work with kids?" Her tone was filled with wonder, and I smiled tenderly.

"You'd be surprised how much I remember," I teased with a wink. She blushed, and I shifted my stance to hopefully hide my raging hard on. "As incredible as you look with that baby in your arms, let Pandora take her and go get your things."

Blair's expression clouded with confusion and a little fear. "Are you ending my internship?"

"Absolutely not," I denied with a shake of my head. "But you're done for tonight." My eyes drifted to Pandora, and I cocked my head towards Blair. The manager hurried over and scooped the baby from Blair's arms.

Once again, that same longing lingered in her eyes as she watched them walk away.

"Patience, bunny," I murmured; then nearly groaned at the memories of saying that to her in my fantasies. We needed to get the fuck out of there so I could sink into her barely legal pussy and give her the baby she so desperately wanted. "Go get your backpack, Blair. We're leaving."

"I'm leaving with you?" She was clearly perplexed by what was happening, but now wasn't the time to explain it in detail so I just nodded. "Where are we going?" she asked.

"To celebrate your birthday." It was the absolute truth. We were going to celebrate with a special dinner at home, and then I was going to commemorate the day she became mine by popping her teenage cherry. "Hurry, bunny." I encouraged her by turning her around and giving her a pat on her deliciously rounded ass.

She glanced back at me over her shoulder. Her eyes were round with shock, but she was silent as she ducked into the classroom. A minute later, she was back at my side with her backpack slung over one shoulder, and I immediately took it from her. Blair looked up at me through her lashes and smiled sweetly. "Thank you."

I returned her smile and gave her long ponytail a playful tug. "Anything for my girl." She looked like she wanted to say something, even opened her mouth but shut it after a beat. "Let's go." I held the front door of the daycare open and gestured for her to walk in front of me. My intentions were chivalrous, but I didn't waste the opportunity to watch her wide hips and perfect ass sway as she sashayed through the lobby and out of the building.

Benjamin was waiting at the curb, lounging against the black limousine and scanning his surroundings. When he spotted us, his eyes swept over Blair, making me clench my jaw and remind myself that I'd scare Blair if I beat the shit out of him in front of her. I was also grateful that she had changed out of her school uniform. While it was sexy as hell and I had every intention of fucking her in it, I didn't like anyone else seeing her that way. The day she graduated would be the last time she wore it in front of anyone but me.

Benjamin grinned and gave me a chin lift before opening the back door. I glared at him when he moved to help her into the car, and he backed off with a smirk. Once she was inside and out of earshot, I leaned close and threatened in a low tone, "Eyes to yourself B and lose the smirk before I permanently disfigure that pretty-boy face of yours." Benjamin smoothed out his expression, but his eyes still danced with laughter.

Choosing to ignore him, I slid onto the black

leather bench seat, and he shut the door behind me. I blinked a few times to let my eyes adjust to the darkened interior, but I didn't have to see Blair to know she was only a few inches away.

I dropped my head back and closed my eyes, trying to relax for a minute as the car glided into traffic. If I didn't get myself under control, I was going to end up with her riding my dick the whole way home. As appealing as the idea was, I refused to take Blair for the first time in the back of a car. Besides, the rug burns from fucking her on the floor would sting like a bitch.

"Justice?"

Her sweet voice warmed me all over, and the sound of my name falling from her perfect mouth caused a smile to crease my face. I opened my eyes and turned my head to gaze at her. Her hands were fidgeting in her lap, and I stilled them by covering them with one of my own. "Yes?"

My attitude must have eased some of her anxiety because she returned my smile and the tension left her hands. "Where are we going?"

"Home, bunny. We're going home."

She canted her head, and her cute little nose scrunched as she thought about my answer. "But you said we were going to celebrate."

Unable to stand the distance any longer, I

cupped her hips and dragged her over until she was sitting astride me. Even in the darkness of the car, I could see her flush as she bit her bottom lip. There was some shyness to her reaction, but I was more interested in the heat sparking in her baby blues. Gently, I pried her lip free before giving in to one of my fantasies and taking it between my own teeth.

Blair gasped, and her hands flew from her lap to clutch my biceps. I nibbled on her lip, then licked the velvety brim to soothe the sting. She moaned, and my cock jumped, startling her when she felt the movement beneath her.

"We are, bunny. We're just going to do it at home," I clarified softly. My lips roved over her silky skin, nibbling and kissing all along her jaw and down her neck. "Our home."

She gasped and started to tremble as her grip on my arms tightened. I swiftly raised my head to search her face and almost let out an audible sigh when I saw only hope shining in her blue pools.

"Our?" she echoed.

I nodded, and my hands traveled around until I was palming her ass. Then I jerked her forward so that her pussy was plastered against the straining bulge in my slacks. "I told you that in thirty days you would be mine." The words were raspy from the effort it was taking to keep from coming. I didn't want to waste a single drop of my sperm. Until she was carrying our baby, I was only going to come inside her.

Once that mission was completed, then I'd start on all of my other fantasies. I was going to fuck her tits before coming all over them. Then I was going to put her on her knees and teach her how to suck my dick deep in her throat before swallowing everything I had to give her.

I groaned and shouted at myself in my head to get my shit together. Today was not the day to let my little head rule me.

Blair had practically melted into me, and I buried my face in the crook of her neck. "All mine, bunny." My tongue darted out for a tiny lick, and I bit back a moan at her fruity taste. I was suddenly starving and wanted to feast by licking every inch of her skin

"Why, um, why do you call me bunny?"

I smiled against her skin and gave her a swift kiss on her collarbone before straightening my back so I could gaze down into her beautiful face. "Because you're so sweet and shy," I told her with a lopsided smile. "I'm betting you're a cuddler, too." Blair giggled and ducked her head, but not before I saw her lips tip up and pink dust her cheeks.

I placed a long finger under her chin and tilted

her head back so I could see her entire face. "There's another reason why bunny so naturally fit you in my mind." It had been a fleeting thought the first time I called her that in my head, but it lurked in the back of my mind whenever I used her nickname.

Blair stared at me, waiting for me to elucidate and part of me wanted to kiss her while I did it. The other, stronger part, wanted to watch her face as I told her, "Because we're going to fuck like bunnies until you're breeding."

Chapter 8
JUSTICE

Heat and excitement flared in Blair's eyes as she stared at me with an open mouth, and I suppressed a triumphant grin. I waited for her to digest my announcement and after a minute, she squeaked, "You want to get me pregnant?" I hadn't considered how fucking sexy it would be to hear her say that. My cock was so swollen that I wasn't sure how much longer my zipper would be able to contain it.

My hands drifted up her back, and I jerked my head from side to side once. "I *am going* to get you pregnant, little bunny."

Before either of us could say another word, we were startled by a sharp rap on the window. A quick glance to my right revealed that we'd arrived at our building. I'd been so wrapped up in Blair that I hadn't noticed the car slowing and coming to a complete stop.

I kissed Blair on the forehead, then grasped her waist and lifted her off of my lap. With one knuckle, I tapped the glass to let Benjamin know we were ready. My other hand wrapped firmly around one of Blair's.

The door opened and I scooted out, then helped Blair alight next to me. Benjamin kept his eyes averted and I grunted in approval, glad to see that he'd taken me seriously.

"I've set up interviews for you tomorrow," I informed him. "I'll let you handle finding your replacement." He nodded and I gave him a small wave, my mind already somewhere else.

My legs were much longer than Blair's, and I was in a huge fucking hurry. To avoid forcing her to run to keep up, I just swept her up into my arms and strode into our building.

On the elevator ride up to the penthouse floor, Blair asked me if I was firing Benjamin. I explained to her that he was hiring me a new security detail because she was now his top priority. I focused hard on the conversation because it was the only thing keeping me from taking her up against the wall. Though it was definitely on the "to do" list for another time.

It wasn't until we were finally inside our apartment with the door shut and locked that I realized the weight I'd been carrying around. While my shoulders felt ten times lighter, my damn cock felt ten times heavier. I needed to get inside her before I nutted in my pants.

The dining room was set up for a birthday party, complete with streamers, balloons, and a shit ton of presents. I'd had every intention of waiting until after dinner, cake, and presents, but reality smacked me in the face and I walked right past, headed straight for our bedroom.

"I promise we'll have a party later, bunny," I told her with only a trace of regret. "I can't wait another minute to see this body I've been fantasizing about for so long. And if I'm going to knock you up tonight, I should probably get an early start." I set her down beside the bed and cupped her face tenderly in my hands. She wore a glazed expression, passion-filled and hungry.

I swallowed hard as I did something I'd been dreaming of for years. Cradling the back of her skull with one hand, I used the other to draw the rubber band down her hair and tossed it aside. I'd never seen her wear her hair down. Staring at it now, floating around her shoulders and tumbling down her back, I was filled with relief that she always wore it up. If any other man ever saw her like this, they'd fight me to the death for this stunning creature.

My eyes moved on to roam over her facial features, admiring her beauty for a few beats before I lowered my head. Our lips touched and when I licked the seam and she immediately opened for me, the world seemed to shift under my feet. Everything came together in complete harmony. Our first kiss was more than I could even imagine. Sparks flew and fire raced from my mouth straight to my dick. She tasted like peaches, and I couldn't get enough.

"I'll be gentle, Blair," I promised in a raspy voice. "But I've waited so long, this first time is going to be fast." She moaned in response, and I wasn't sure if she even really comprehended what I was saying.

Not more than a few minutes later, I had us both stripped and Blair laid out on the center of our bed. "Your curves are even more mouthwatering that I realized," I grunted as I took a moment to admire her form. I straddled her thighs and cupped her full-sized tits. "These are perfect for nursing babies. And, giant enough to feed me too." I couldn't wait to taste her sweet nipple juice. Bending down, I sucked on each of her large nipples in turn. Blair's hands dove into her hair, clenching the strands as she wiggled and moaned from my ministrations.

Next, I latched onto her hips and leaned down to place a kiss on each one. "Wide and open, made for taking me deep and carrying our babies. Fuck, bunny," I breathed reverently. "Your body was created for baby-making." I moved back until I was kneeling between her knees and ran my palms up her legs. I stopped when I reached her thick thighs and licked my lips as I stared at her bare, glistening pussy. "I'm going to have you lasered so there will never be anything between us," I told her as I petted her mound. She squirmed, and I dipped a finger between her folds and ran it over her clit before slowly pushing it inside her virgin hole.

"Fuck!" I cursed as I worked the digit in. She was so fucking snug that I had no doubt the squeeze would be a little painful on my dick, but it would be completely worth it. And, it meant her pussy would milk it and suck up every drop of my seed.

"You want a baby, don't you, Blair?" I purred as I moved my finger in and out. She moaned and nodded, her legs instinctively spreading farther apart. "I know you do. I've watched you every day, and I saw how you looked at those babies, bunny.

It's all you've ever wanted, isn't it? To be a mommy?"

Blair's eyes widened just a fraction, showing her surprise at either my stalking or my perceptiveness. I wasn't sure which. But when her inner walls clamped down on my finger, I took it as a sign that she wanted me to continue.

"Don't worry, bunny. I'm going to give you what you want. What we both want." I slipped a second finger in and stretched her muscles, getting her ready to take my fat cock. "Once I pop your cherry, I'm going to fuck you until I've given you all of my come. Then, when you've had time to rest, I'm going to mount you like a fucking animal until you've made me a daddy."

Blair whimpered, and her pelvis bucked up to meet my finger thrusts. I knew she'd be softer and more open if she came first, so I scooted down onto my belly and shoved my face in her sex. My mouth licked and bit at her clit while my hand pumped. My whiskers brushing over her soft skin only seemed to drive her even more crazy. When she was writhing and crying out my name, right on the edge, I drew my fingers out. She started to whine in protest, but it became a keening wail when I replaced my fingers with my stiffened tongue and speared in and out of her channel as I plucked her little pleasure button like the strings of a violin. Her flavor burst on my tongue, and I wondered if I was turning blue from the effort not to come. My balls probably looked like giant blueberries.

Blair's whole body froze for a beat, even her breathing had stalled. Then she threw back her head and screamed as she came with a series of violent shudders.

While her body was pulsing with her orgasm, I pushed back up onto my knees and pressed Blair's legs as wide as they would go. I lined up my cock with her entrance, then stopped as a thought came to me.

My hand darted out and I grasped her chin tightly, forcing her to look at me. "Did you stay off the pill like I told you to?" I demanded. She swallowed hard as she tried to focus on my words, but she was struggling since she was basically mid-orgasm. "Did you keep your body pure and ripe for me, Blair?"

She finally managed a nod, and I smiled as I caressed her face. "Good girl, bunny. You're ovulating so your body is primed and ready, just begging to be filled. There's nothing stopping me from putting my baby inside your soft belly." I snatched a pillow from the top of the bed and slid it under her hips.

I leaned forward and took hold of her wrists, pulling her hands from her hair and bring them down to her pussy. "Hold it open for me, baby," I instructed her. Her cheeks reddened through the pink flush of her heated skin, but she did as she was told. She used the fingers of each hand to open her folds, baring her soaked, pink flesh. Her clit was swollen and hard, making it pop out of its hood.

I watched intently as I slipped the engorged tip of my cock in her tight heat and then groaned at the snug fit. I gritted my teeth in an effort to be gentle as I sunk in a little more until I hit her innocence.

"Knowing that this pussy is untouched and I'm the only man who will ever feel its blissful grip is hot as fuck," I growled as I broke through Blair's barrier with one hard thrust. I gave her a little time to adjust to my size, but her shudders had subsided, and her heart rate was quickly decelerating. I wanted to come in her while her cervix was soft, so I started to move as soon as I felt she could handle it.

"Justice," she moaned.

It was like throwing gasoline on a blazing inferno. "Say it again," I snarled as I picked up my pace, practically pounding her into the mattress.

"Justice."

"Fuck, I love hearing you say my name while I'm rutting inside your pussy."

I was getting too close and needed to make sure she came again when I blew so that her womb was open. Sliding my hands under her ass, I lifted her up so I could go deeper and hit her clit with every pass. "Fuck!" I shouted when her walls clamped down hard. It hurt like hell, but the pain heightened my ecstasy and caused me to go off like a fucking rocket. I shoved in as far as I could go until my dick hit her cervix, and her pussy lips wrapped tight around it.

Blair's body froze, strung tight for a couple of seconds before she screamed and shattered. Her pussy convulsed around my cock as she came, sucking me dry. "Such a good little girl," I crooned as I rocked into her, the small movement enough to draw out her orgasm but not enough to actually break the seal.

I wanted nothing more than to clamp my legs around hers, roll to my back, and fall asleep buried in my baby girl's pussy. But judging from how tight she was, I knew it would cause her to be sore longer and I wanted her to heal as quickly as possible. I hated the thought of her hurting…and I couldn't wait to get back to making babies.

Slowly, I withdrew and though she clenched her

legs to keep me from leaving, she also whimpered in pain. "Let me take care of you, bunny."

I climbed off the bed and jogged to the master bath, my dick bouncing because while I'd softened just a touch, I was still fully erect. A stack of washcloths sat folded on a shelf in between the double sinks. I lifted the top one off the pile and ran it under warm water.

My cock was covered in her sweet cream and it had a pink tinge to it, proof that I'd made her a woman. I hesitated to wipe it off, wanting to wear the proof like a badge of honor. However, I was afraid Blair might realize just how bat-shit-crazy I was if she saw me coveting her virgin blood. I needed to make sure she was madly in love with me, wearing my ring, and carrying our baby before she saw the true extent of my obsession with her. Otherwise, it might send her running. Not that she'd get far. I wasn't ever going to let her go. If she got freaked, she'd come around eventually.

After cleaning myself up, I took a fresh, wet cloth back to the bed and tenderly washed between her legs. "You're pretty red, bunny," I sighed. "Shit. I shouldn't have taken you so hard your first time."

Blair drew my attention by placing a hand on my arm. "It was perfect," she whispered when our eyes met. There was nothing but sincerity in her blue depths.

"I'm happy you feel that way." Our lips met in a sweet kiss, then I pressed her back down onto the bed. I made sure she was still situated with the pillow angling her hips up, then crawled in and laid down beside her. I put one arm under her head and cupped one of her ample tits with my free hand, then threw one leg over both of hers. "It just means I'll have to get creative for the next day or so," I murmured sleepily.

"Creative?" she sounded amused, and it brought a smile to my lips.

"Creative ways to fill your pussy with my come without hurting you," I explained. Then my tone turned cocky. "Don't worry, I have endless ideas when it comes to your body, bunny."

Chapter 9
JUSTICE

When I woke from our nap, Blair was awake and studying me with a worried expression while she chewed on her bottom lip.

"Don't, Blair," I admonished. "I'm the only one who gets to bite that lip." Yep. I was jealous of fucking teeth.

I brushed loose strands of straight blonde hair back from her face. "What's going on in that head of yours, bunny?"

"What is this?" she asked timidly.

"This?" I raised a brow. "You're going to need to be a little more specific. And I'm going to assume you aren't talking about my dick because that would just be insulting."

Blair giggled, but the smile didn't quite reach her eyes. "I meant, this—you know—us."

I leaned up on my elbow so I could see all of her face while we talked. "That's it. Us."

She looked confused by my answer.

"You"—I pointed at her chest—"me"—I pointed at my own chest and then at her tummy—"and baby makes three. For now."

Blair laughed, and the beautiful bell-like sound warmed my heart and hardened my cock. "So, I'm your baby momma?" She asked it flippantly, but as usual, she wore her true feelings on her face, and I could clearly see that she was afraid I was going to say yes.

"Bunny." I turned her on her side so we were facing each other. "Don't ever refer to yourself like that again. You are the mother of my children—"

"As in plural?" she interrupted with a squeak. Her face flushed with delight, clearly liking the idea.

"I intend to keep you pregnant for a long time," I stated. "You're going to be too irresistible when you're wearing my ring and dripping milk from your sexy tits." I licked my lips in anticipation as I eyed her chest hungrily.

"Justice?"

"I fucking love the way you say my name," I sighed.

"Justice, focus!" she snapped.

My head flew up in surprise, and I grinned at

the glimpse of her backbone. I loved that my girl was so soft and sweet, but I had a feeling that attitude I glimpsed from time to time would end up making her a tigress in bed.

"What, bunny?"

"Did you say ring?"

I frowned. "Of course, I said ring. You think I'd let my wife walk around without a ring, so every bastard around her knows she's taken?"

Blair tensed and stared at me in silence.

"What?" I finally asked.

She huffed with impatience, and it was cute as fuck.

"Are you going to ask me?"

"Ask you what?"

"To marry you!" she practically shouted.

My brows drew down, and I scowled. "Absolutely not."

Blair sat up and stared down at me incredulously. "You just said you wanted me to have your babies and wear a ring. But we're not getting married?"

I shifted so I was sitting up too before replying. "We are getting married." My tone made it clear this was not up for debate.

Blair shouted in frustration and pulled on her hair. "What the heck are you talking about?

How can we get married if you aren't asking me?"

Ah, then it all made sense. "Bunny, I'm not asking because you have no other choice. We're getting married, and that's final."

"So…." She started ticking off her fingers as she made a list. "I'm moving in"—I nodded—"we're getting married"—another nod—"and I'm apparently going to be baring you a gaggle of babies. Does that about sum it up?"

Her voice held a hint of sarcasm, and I narrowed my eyes while I waited for her to make her point.

"Why? Why do you want all that with me?"

"Because I love you," I said with exasperation.

"Oh."

I laughed at her befuddled expression. She clearly hadn't expected my answer. Although I didn't know how she hadn't figured that out yet. "Bunny, I've loved you since long before I should have." I decided to lay it all out for her. "There are no limits to my obsession with you, Blair. I'm going to be a possessive, jealous, domineering asshole sometimes, but no one will ever love you more than I do."

She clasped her hands in front of her chest, and I was very proud of the fact that I didn't let it draw my eyes down to her tits. "I love you, too," she chirped brightly.

"Good." I gently pushed her shoulder until she was once again lying on her back. "Now, let's work on those babies." After adjusting the pillow, I decided to eat her pussy until she came, then come all over it and push as much of it as I could inside. After that, I jacked off with my dick inside only an inch or so. Then we fell into another exhausted heap and slept.

It was morning when we woke up next. Actually, she woke me when she dragged me out of bed, having discovered the birthday set up she hadn't noticed the night before.

She opened her presents, the last one being a little blue box that contained a five-carat diamond ring that I slipped on her third, left finger.

While she went into the bedroom to put her new things away, I made my way to the kitchen and served up a huge slice of her cake. When I walked back into the bedroom, she was looking around with a puzzled and slightly amused expression.

She was clearly just noticing that all of her things were already moved in and put away. Talking her dad around to my way of thinking had taken work even though she was going to be right next door, but he'd finally caved when he realized I wasn't going to budge. But, that was all forgotten when she spotted the plate in my hand. Her eyes lit up like a kid on Christmas morning.

I swaggered over to her, and she reached for it but I held it away. "You can have some cake, but I'm going to feed it to you."

She opened her mouth, and I smirked. "Nope. We're going to eat it my way."

She quickly learned that my way meant I fed her some cake and ate the rest off of her body. After licking most of the frosting from her pussy, I buried my eleven inches to the hilt and filled her like a Twinkie with my own thick, sticky cream.

Epilogue 1
JUSTICE

Almost 2 years later...

Sweet milk splashed in my mouth as my orgasm barreled through me. I sucked hard on her nipple, hungry for more as my hips punched up while my wife rode my cock and cried out my name. "Gently, bunny," I cautioned her as I stroked her swollen belly.

Sucking Blair's milky tits while I fucked her always made me come so hard, I nearly passed the fuck out. And, it made Blair turn wild. Her nipples had been extremely sensitive when she'd been pregnant with our son. I'd often made her come just from playing with them. But when she got pregnant with our daughter two months after Trevor was born, we'd discovered that knocked up and nursing was a lethal combination for Blair. I could give her orgasm after orgasm, right on the heels of each other by slamming my cock into her pregnant pussy and lavishing attention on her incredible breasts. So far, we'd gotten to five before she shoved me away and swore if I came near her again, she'd have her tubes tied after this baby.

I'd laughed because we both knew that pregnant Blair was horny all the time and she'd be begging for it soon enough. I was determined to get her to six one of these days.

"So?" she asked when we were sprawled out next to each other in bed, content and satisfied.

I grinned when I looked down to see her watching me through her lashes, twin pink spots blooming on her cheeks.

"There is no comparison," I declared quietly. "My fantasies have never lived up to the real thing."

Blair grinned and turned her head to kiss my chest, then raised her eyes to mine again. "What's the score now?"

I laughed and dragged her into my arms. "I've lost count, bunny." When Blair found my duffel of towels in the back of the town car one day, I ended up confessing to her about my morning fantasies. To my surprise, she wanted to know if she would trump my dreams of her. It came as no shock to me when she blew them away every single time.

"What's next?" she asked eagerly, and I chuckled.

"How about we stop trying to outdo what isn't real and focus on trying new things?"

Blair scratched her fingers down the whiskers on my face, making me shiver, and gave me a wicked grin. "Like the time we decided to see if the skin under your goatee was particularly sensitive?"

Yeah, turned out that was quite an erogenous zone for me. Go figure.

"How about we see if I can pump enough come into your pussy to turn this pregnancy into twins?" I teased.

"Good grief." She rolled her eyes playfully. "Then I'd be nursing two babies at once! My boobs would be huge!"

I cupped her tits and squeezed, then leaned down to lick them clean, making Blair moan. "Don't worry, bunny." I winked. "I'll eat their leftovers."

Blair arched her back, thrusting her breasts into my face and whimpered. "More," she begged.

Before I could give her what she wanted, a high-pitched wail came out of the baby monitor on the bedside table.

"Fuck," I groaned as I rested my forehead in the valley between her tits.

Blair giggled and moved to get out of bed, but I held her back with a hand on her shoulder. "Stay here, bunny. I'll bring him in."

After she fed the baby, we played with him until he fell back asleep. Blair and I watched him for a few minutes, enjoying the life we'd made for ourselves. I stood behind her with my hands resting on her growing belly. We only had around eight weeks left before we'd meet our daughter.

Once the doc gave her the "all clear" I was honest enough with myself to know that the Neanderthal wouldn't be too far in the shadows. She'd more than likely be bred again by the time our baby girl was three months old.

I removed one of my hands but kept the other on Blair's waist and guided her next door to our room. I flipped on the monitor and shut the door before going to work on removing Blair's clothes.

"About trying new things…" I trailed off, and she gave me a sassy look, making me laugh. "I'd like to get back to the attempt to turn one baby into two." I flashed her a cheesy grin, and she giggled.

"You just want to go for six," she argued.

"That should do it, don't' you think?"

Blair rolled her eyes. "I think five's my limit, babe."

I proved her wrong on two counts.

First, I got her to seven.

Second, it seemed turning one baby into two wasn't as impossible as it seemed.

After Blair delivered our daughter, the doctor blanched while looking at the computer screen, then yelled for the staff to get ready for another one.

They told us that little Jenna had been hiding Dani, and no one had realized it was twins until the birth.

I still maintained that it was the seventh orgasm.

Epilogue 2
BLAIR

Four and a half years later...

Watching Justice play with our children was one of my favorite things. He was such a great father. Justice was involved in every aspect of the kids' lives. K-Corp was more successful than ever, but he and Thatcher had quickly learned how to delegate to make time for what was important to them.

Justice even took over Trevor's t-ball team last year...after he got into it with the coach for supposedly flirting with me. I hadn't noticed anything inappropriate, but Justice insisted that the guy kept staring at me and had to go. I didn't argue since his possessive displays gave me a little thrill. It also didn't hurt that Trevor thought having his daddy as his coach was the best thing ever.

Of course, that led to his sisters complaining because Justice wasn't their coach too. The twins were four, and they weren't used to hearing no very often since they had their daddy and big brother wrapped around their little fingers. Rubbing my rounded belly, my lips curved up in a smile as I thought about how much Jenna and Dani had pestered their tumbling class teacher until she agreed that I could assist her.

But that had only lasted a few months before we found out we were expecting our fourth child. Justice tended to treat me like I was breakable when I was pregnant—except when he lost control in bed. And even then it was only to a certain extent. He didn't let go quite as much as normal.

Justice definitely didn't trust a bunch of rambunctious preschoolers to roll around on the mats with me. Especially not when he'd waited three years to knock me up again so I could finish my bachelor's degree. It'd been difficult with three babies at home, and I'd only managed it because of Justice's support. He wanted me to have everything I desired, and I'd learned early on in our relationship that he'd go to whatever lengths needed to make sure I got it. Not that he found taking the kids to the in-house daycare at K-Corp a hardship. Quite the contrary, he loved being able to pop in to see them throughout the day. And now that I was done with school, I was on site too because I'd taken over the running of the daycare so Pandora could retire. It was the perfect job for me, surrounded by kids—including all of my own until Trevor started kindergarten in the fall—and close to my husband.

"Help us get Daddy," the twins screeched in unison.

"Noooooo," Justice cried when Trevor switched sides and teamed up with the girls to reach up and tickle his sides and belly.

I'd been watching from the doorway of their playroom without any of them noticing me, but then a giggle slipped past my lips when Justice staggered backwards and crashed to the floor in an exaggerated fall. All four heads turned in my direction, and big grins split their precious faces.

"Wanna tickle Daddy, too?" Trevor offered, his gray eyes twinkling with delight. "I'll hold him down so he can't get you back."

"Yeah, Dani and me can grab his arms," Jenna added, climbing over Justice's body to wrap her little hands around his left bicep.

Dani mirrored her action, throwing her body over Justice's right arm. "C'mon, Mommy! Get 'im!"

"How can I pass up an offer like that?" I laughed as I moved forward.

"Don't move, Daddy. We have to be careful with Mommy since she's pregnant," Trevor warned, mimicking what Justice had told the kids about a million times over the past few months as he held his legs down.

Justice craned his neck up to meet Trevor's gaze as he said, "Thanks for the reminder, buddy."

I barely held in my snort at Justice's response as I lowered myself to my knees next to him. He didn't need anyone to caution him when it came to me since he'd wrap me in bubble wrap if he could. And then I'd just have to get him all worked up until he couldn't wait to rip it right back off.

When my fingers brushed against his stomach before heading to his sides, Justice's eyes darkened to a stormy gray, and a low groan bubbled up his throat. I couldn't torture him too much with the kids so close, but I also couldn't resist the temptation to cop a feel of his abs when they were right there in front of me. Not with my pregnancy hormones raging through my system, or at least that was the excuse I was going with.

Before we got any awkward questions about the sudden tightness of his jeans, I aimed for an especially ticklish spot just under his rib cage. When he roared with laughter, the kids wanted a turn too. By the time we were done, we were all laughing so hard that our sides hurt.

"Alright, guys. I think Mommy has had enough tickle time and needs a snack. How do cookies and milk sound to everyone?" Justice asked.

"Cookies! Yay!" the kids cheered, scrambling to their feet to race towards the kitchen.

"I'll get you back for that later," Justice murmured against my ear after helping me up from the floor so we could follow after them.

"You'd better," I whispered back with a wink, looking forward to some quality alone time when the kids went down for the night.

My life was better than I'd dreamed it would be in my wildest dreams about Justice. But just like he'd told me a million times about his fantasies, reality far surpassed my imagination.

CURIOUS ABOUT THATCHER? Her Love is now available! Want a FREE copy of The Virgin's Guardian? Sign up for our mailing list now!

Epilogue 3
BLAIR

"What's wrong, Mommy?"

"Nothing, baby," I answered distractedly as I tried to concentrate on Trevor's at-bat while rubbing my lower back. "I'm just watching your brother."

Dani reached behind me to put her little hand over mine. "Do you haf an owie?"

Jenna cuddled into my other side and frowned up at me. "Are you sick, Mommy?"

Their questions caught Imogene's attention, and she leaned over Dani to stare at me. Her gaze dropped to my rounded belly after she took in the grimace on my face. Bending closer, she hissed, "Are you in labor?"

"Maybe," I mumbled.

"How long has this been going on?" Imogene

asked as she twisted around to hand their youngest over to Thatcher.

"My back has been hurting since I woke up this morning. At first, I thought it was just normal pregnancy stuff." I pointed at my stomach. "You'd think that since I'm only carrying one girl this time that I wouldn't be so big, but nope. I'm huge, and my back aches so much I was starting to wonder if they missed another baby again. Not that it could be possible with the number of ultrasounds Justice had them do this time around just so we wouldn't be surprised again."

Imogene held up her hand to stop the never-ending flow of my words. "Whoa! You're getting off track. You don't have to tell me how many aches and pains there are when you're pregnant. After having four babies in four years, I know. But you do need to tell me if your back pain has turned into contractions."

"Yes," I panted as my belly tightened and a wave of pain crashed over me.

Her head reared back in shock, and she jumped up. "Seriously? You're just sitting there in labor? What're you waiting for, the game to end?"

I nodded jerkily, unable to get any words out at the moment.

"Daddy!" Dani and Jenna screamed in unison.

Justice was standing in the dugout to the left of home plate, and his head whipped in their direction as soon as he heard his daughter's voices.

"Mommy's hafin' the baby!" Jenna explained.

"Now!" Dani added.

"Damn, it's a good thing you're giving my brother another baby," Thatcher sighed, shaking his head as he stood and started to gather all of our things. "The recovery process just might be long enough that he'll have time to get over being pissed that you didn't have one of us get him as soon as you started having contractions."

'Only if you make it to the hospital and don't have the baby in the car," Imogene pointed out as Justice raced over to the stands. "If that happens, he'll never let you live it down."

"And you'll probably end up with a red ass as soon as the doctor says you're fully healed," Thatcher mumbled under his breath just loud enough for Imogene and me to hear.

It was my face that turned red and not because of the strain from the contraction that ended seconds before my husband reached me. I could too easily picture him spanking my backside, and it was awkward to get a little turned on by the thought while I was in labor.

"C'mon, bunny. I've got you," Justice

murmured as he wrapped his arm around my waist to help me stand. Once I was on my feet, he glanced to the right and nodded. "Benjamin is going to get the car, so you don't have far to walk. Will you be okay, or do you need me to carry you?"

"I can walk," I grumbled as he kept his arm around me and took most of my weight anyway.

"We'll take the kids," Thatcher offered.

"Take us where? Why did Dad come over here when I was hitting a home run?" Trevor asked, his eyes narrowing when he spotted how Justice was holding me. "What's wrong with Mommy?"

"I'm okay, sweetie," I reassured my little protector.

Thatcher patted his shoulder and explained, "Your dad is going to take your mom to the hospital so she can have the baby, and you guys are going to come with us."

"That's not going to work. Your SUV is big, but no way will it fit all the booster and car seats you'd need for this crew," Justice said, calling attention to the logistical issue of having seven kids between the two couples as he started to lead me around the stands.

"Kya has a vehicle with her, so we have enough room for everybody," Thatcher assured him.

"Perfect." Justice ran his hand through his hair,

heaving a sigh of relief. "You take the kids, and I'll call when there's news."

"Nuh-uh." Trevor shook his head. "I'm going with Mommy. She might need me."

"I won't let anything happen to her." Justice let go of me to bend down to our son's level. "But I need you to help look after your sisters for me. Can you do that, buddy?"

Trevor's chest puffed up, and he nodded. "Yup, I'll make sure they're okay."

"We'll get the kids cleaned up and fed, and then we'll head over to the hospital so Trevor, Dani, and Jenna can meet their baby sister as soon as she's here," Imogene offered, flashing a grin at my son. "Since we all know Trevor is going to pester us to head over there before too long."

My laughter turned into a gasp when my stomach tightened again, the pain hitting me hard. I reached out and placed my hand on Justice's shoulder to steady myself. I held on until the contraction passed. "We need to go. Now."

Everybody trailed after us and watched as Justice got me settled into one of the captain's chairs in the second row of our Cadillac Escalade. While he ran around to the other side, Benjamin grabbed my overnight bag—which Justice had put back there a week ago just in case we needed it—

from the back and tossed it in the passenger seat. We roared out of the parking lot, but it didn't matter that Benjamin drove ten miles over the speed limit. It turned out that Imogene had jinxed us by bringing up how angry Justice would be if we didn't make it to the hospital. I would've had the baby in the car if Benjamin hadn't called for an ambulance on our way there. But at least there was only one this time—a beautiful girl we named Samantha—even if Justice did spank my butt before fucking me hard from behind so he could see his handprint after my six-week appointment.

Epilogue 4
JUSTICE

Blair sniffled, and I gently smiled as I slipped my arm around her and pulled her close. Trevor waved excitedly, then spun around and raced into the school with his friends. "He'll be okay," I assured her softly.

"My baby is all grown up," she wailed as tears streamed down her face. She turned in my embrace and buried her face in my shirt as she sobbed. I hated to see her cry, and a part of me felt the same way. So I hurried to comfort her, hoping I'd believe my own words.

"It's just first grade, bunny," I reminded her with a kiss to the crown of her head.

"He'll be driving tomorrow and graduating next week, and the next thing you know, he'll be getting married and won't be my little boy anymore."

I couldn't help fighting a chuckle because she was so fucking adorable. "Trevor will always be your baby, Blair."

"No, he won't," she sniffled again, no longer crying. "His heart will belong to some girl and...and.." I could tell she was ramping up for another round of sobs, so I tried a different tactic.

"Then he'll have babies of his own, and you'll be able to spoil them rotten."

Just as I'd hoped, her head popped up, and she stared up at me with red-rimmed, yet still amazing blue eyes. A tiny smile played at the corners of her mouth, and she hiccuped once before it grew. "Grandbabies?"

I laughed and squeezed her in a bear hug. "Just think, you'll get to spoil them and send them right back to their parents."

"That will be so fun," she gushed, her mind sufficiently distracted from her sorrow over Trevor starting first grade. Then she sighed. "That's a long way off, though. At least I have Eva to get my baby cuddles." She frowned slightly, and another little sigh escaped. "She's almost one, Justice. She won't be a baby for very long." Her eyes filled with fresh tears, and I kissed her. A long, passionate mating of our mouths to give her something else to think about.

Like always, the heat between us flared red hot, and I instantly grew hard as steel. Before things could get out of hand, I tore my lips from my wife's and guided her swiftly to our car. Once we were inside, I dragged her onto my lap and picked up where we'd left off.

Most of the blood in my brain had rushed down to my groin, but there was just enough left to recognize that she was ready, even if she hadn't realized it yet.

"YES!" Blaire cried out as she dropped down onto my long, thick cock. Her large, round tits bounced, leaking droplets of milk onto my chest.

"Thirsty," I grunted. I wasn't about to waste any more of her nectar, so I gripped her hips and surged up to take one swollen nipple in my mouth. I swallowed around the hard peak, drawing out more and greedily feeding from her milky tits.

Blair's head dropped back, and she cried out, her movements becoming faster and more frantic. "Shhhh, bunny," I mumbled. "Don't wake our babies." I switched to the other breast, and she whimpered. The kids were all down for the night, which was rare when you had five. So we were taking full advantage of our alone time.

I glanced up to see her biting her lip, her eyes tightly closed, and her face flushed pink, all the way down her chest. Fuck. She was so gorgeous. Every day that we were together, she grew more and more beautiful. But I reached out and pulled her lip from between her teeth. I stopped moving and glared at her. "You know I don't like it when someone else bites your lips," I reminded her. She nodded, and when I didn't resume moving right away, she pouted adorably and squeezed her walls around my dick.

"Your body is hungry for my cock, isn't it, bunny?" I rasped as streaks of pleasure shot through me.

"Justice," she breathed. Hearing her say my name while I was fucking her always pushed me so close to the edge. Her pussy had me in a fucking death grip, and when she spasmed, I forgot about being quiet and shouted, "Fuck, yes!" Blair slapped her hand over my mouth and giggled until I yanked her down hard and circled my pelvis, hitting all the right spots. "I'm not going to last, bunny," I growled. "Tighten that sweet pussy and take me deeply while you come." Despite five kids and having just turned twenty-five, Blair was tight as fuck and had the ability to make me lose my mind when she came around my cock. "I want you to take every drop of my seed, Blair," I demanded. "I want to be a daddy one more time."

After we had Samantha, Blair had sworn up and down that she was done. A year and a half later, she'd begged me to put another baby inside her while I was fucking her fast and hard against my office wall in an attempt to distract her from the twins starting preschool. I wasn't about to argue since I wanted more children and loved seeing my woman round and swollen with the proof that she was mine.

Then we had Eva, and she swore that was it, but I still wanted one more. Blair loved nothing more than being a wife and a mother, and I knew she'd always wanted six kids. After sending her oldest off to first grade that morning, I had a feeling she was ready. It was perfect timing too. My mind seemed to naturally keep track of her cycles since the day I'd seen that tampon in her purse when she was sixteen. And my girl was ripe and fertile, ready for me to knock her up.

"I know you want another baby. Admit it, bunny." Her pussy clenched, and she moaned, making me smile. Without warning, I flipped her over and shoved her legs up, resting them on my shoulders. Then I plunged back in, bottoming out so my tip pressed into her cervix. "I'm going to pump you full of my cream, baby," I growled as I retreated just a little, then drove back in and started pounding deep and hard, rutting in her like an animal with its mate. "Oh, fuck. Fuck, yes." I grabbed her hands which had been clenched in the sheets and brought them to the apex of her thighs. "You know what I want, bunny."

Blair moaned and bucked her hips as her hands slid down, and her fingers pulled her lips apart, giving me an unobstructed view of her pink, needy pussy. "It gets me so fucking hot when you obey me, baby. Now, I want you to come, so your womb sucks up every fucking drop."

Blair's head twisted side to side, and she widened her legs, so they dropped and hung over my arms. Her body was perfect for giving me babies, with wide hips and big tits. But she'd also grown curvier with each pregnancy, and it was sexy as fuck. "That's right, bunny. Open up for me."

She cried out softly while thrusting her pelvis up as I slammed back in. "Yes," she whimpered. "Give it to me, Justice. Oh, oh! Yes! Yes!" She pressed her head back into the mattress, her mouth open in a silent scream as she shattered.

"Good girl," I praised on a grunt when I felt her cervical wall soften, letting me in even deeper.

I watched my cock, shiny from her juices, sink back in one last time as I gave myself over to my climax. "Oh, yeah. Fuck yes, bunny. Fuck!" My voice was gravelly from my clenched jaw. I was trying to hold back my desire to bellow as hot, thick come jetted from my shaft, filling her to the brim. Blair shivered and quaked from the force of her orgasm, but her muscles were tightening as she drew near to another peak. The sight pushed out even more of my seed. "That's it, bunny," I grunted as I rocked into her over and over. "Come again, baby. I want to make sure you're stuffed full." I removed her hands so that her folds sealed around my cock, preventing much from slipping out.

I made her come twice more before collapsing onto the bed, careful not to crush her. I wrapped my legs around hers and rolled to my back, keeping us connected. I fully intended to spend the night buried inside her pussy.

"I love you so fucking much, bunny."

Blair sighed and snuggled into me. "Love you, too, Justice. Always."

I kissed her temple and murmured, "Always."

It was a fucking miracle that all of our children slept through the night because, when I wasn't sleeping, I was rocking into her pussy and playing with her clit while I sucked on her juicy tits until she gave me another orgasm or two.

Knowing I'd fucked her into oblivion and let her get very little sleep, I fed our babies and took them to the park. And a year later, we were at the park again, this time with my beautiful wife curled up beside me and our three-month-old Bianca cradled in my arms.

Her Love

Billionaire Thatcher Kendall had everything a man could want. Money. Success. Fame.

But none of that mattered to him. The only thing he ever desired was the woman who was meant to be his.

When he finally found her, Thatcher was determined to create the perfect home for them before he claimed Imogene as his own.

Prologue
THATCHER

When you were six foot five with a big, muscular frame, you weren't exactly hard to miss. I also had the tall, dark, and handsome thing going on. Not that I was particularly vain, but over the years, my brother, Justice, and I had both made The World's Most Eligible Billionaires list, as well as being categorized in the "Most Sexy" blah blah blah in a dozen magazines. We'd also graced the cover of Forbes magazine multiple times. Apparently, my "dark hair, gray eyes, strong jaw, and full lips" made me desirable and easily noticed.

So, it completely baffled me that I'd been wandering past the woman of my dreams almost every day for the past month and I'd never so much as caught her eye.

Imogene Collier, according to her signature on

her work, was a street artist, usually set up in Battery Park, not far from my office building. The first time I passed by, the smell of cinnamon and sugar had wafted under my nose, and I'd looked around for a food cart only to realize that it was coming from the artist sitting on a stool, painting. I was immediately drawn in by the emotion behind her paintings…until I saw her. Love hit me like a ton of bricks. I couldn't take my eyes off of her, and one word kept bouncing around in my head over and over. *Mine.*

Chapter 1
THATCHER

"There's been a delay in shipping the materials for the renovation, Mr. Kendall."

I cursed and clenched the phone so hard I was surprised it didn't crumble to dust. At least I hadn't chucked it at the glass wall across from my desk like I'd been tempted to do.

Nolan, my assistant, would have been fucking pissed if I cracked the glass, especially because it was right behind his desk. Then he probably would have tattled on me to Patti. I didn't want to face the wrath of the woman who'd been like a mother to me for the past fifteen years. She technically worked for my brother, but the honest truth was that she ran this place and it would fall apart without her.

"How far is it going to push back the project this time?"

"Um, well—we aren't sure. Two weeks, maybe?" he stammered.

"You're fired," I snarled just before I heard the crunch of my phone cracking in my hand. "Fuck," I mumbled when I pulled it away from my ear to inspect the damage.

I pushed to my feet and stalked to my door. Nolan looked up when I came to a stop by his desk. "Headed to your dinner meeting?" he asked as he scribbled something on a planner sitting open before him. Nolan was a true millennial in most ways, but he still clung to some old traditions, like backing up digital calendars with paper ones. I didn't give a shit how he organized things, he never missed anything. If I was late to a meeting, it was my own damn fault, as he would tell me afterward.

"Yes." I tossed the ruined phone into the air, and he instinctively caught it in one hand like I knew he would. He had mad reflexes, and I often wondered if he moonlit as a ninja. "Order me a new phone."

"Hulk smash much?" Nolan quipped with a raised brow.

"And I need to find a new contractor for the renovation on my townhouse," I deflected.

He shook his head as he made notes. "Another delay? Seriously?" His annoyed tone validated my frustration. I wasn't overreacting. "What's that make? Four times?"

"Something like that. This is taking way too fucking long," I growled. "I need it done as soon as possible. I don't care how much it costs, find me someone who can get it done in two weeks."

Nolan sucked in a breath and shook his head. "That's going to set you back a pretty penny."

I shrugged. It wouldn't even put a dent in my checking account, much less the overall total of my assets. "Get it done."

The only reason I'd been able to wait this long was knowing that everything had to be just perfect before I made my move. I was doing everything I could think of to ensure that when I finally went for my girl, I would've done everything I could to earn her love.

I took a deep breath and tried to expel the residual anger from my phone call. My dinner meeting was crucial, and the last thing I needed was to take out my irritation on the man about to merge his business with ours.

I sauntered into Justice's office and leaned against the doorway, shoving my hands in my pockets. Justice was staring intently at his phone, more than likely, stalking his girl.

His head lifted, and he scowled at me before

snapping, "Remind me why this meeting had to happen tonight?"

"Jamison is getting married this weekend, and he'll be gone on his honeymoon for three months," I reminded him. "We need this merger to go through before the fiscal year ends."

"Okayyy," he dragged out the word. "But why a dinner meeting? This couldn't have been done during lunch?"

My gaze had wandered to the floor-to-ceiling windows across the room from me, and I meandered over to them. My eyes dropped down the forty-five floors below us to search out the view of Battery Park. We were too far for me to really see who and what was there. But it didn't stop me from studying the scene in the hope of spotting her. "I'm not available for lunch meetings," I finally responded, scarcely paying him any attention.

After a minute, I felt him walk up beside me, and his curious gaze followed mine. "Want to give me a little more explanation than that, brother?"

I swore and turned away from the window, my hands clenching in my pockets. "She's there," I bit out. "Every day. It's the only time I have to see her." The only time I could fucking breathe lately. Even if we'd never spoken, and she didn't realize I was alive.

Justice's brows shot up to his hairline. It was an understandable reaction; I hadn't told him about Imogene yet. I wasn't completely sure why, if anyone would understand this consuming obsession for their woman, it was Justice. He'd been stalking Blair, the object of his love, for nearly two years. When I found Imogene, I realized I had more in common with my brother than I thought.

"The one," I expounded as I turned my tumultuous gaze in his direction.

Justice contemplated me for a few moments, then asked, "So, what's the problem? Why are you hesitating?"

I shook my head. And that, right there, was the true reason behind my reluctance to confide in him. Justice was forced to wait for Blair because she was still underage. He wouldn't understand my decision. I pulled my hands from my pockets and crossed my arms over my chest. "I'm not hesitating," I disagreed. "I'm just not ready yet. Everything has to be perfect."

"Everything?" he asked, clearly still confused. "What are you waiting for?" The thing was, Justice had passed the time by putting his plans in place. He hadn't considered what he would have done had he met Blair after she'd turned eighteen. I couldn't help but imagine that he would have taken the same path as me and waited for a plan to come together rather than go off half-cocked.

But, now wasn't the time to get into it. "I'll explain another time. We're going to be late."

Justice looked like he wanted to argue, but he stayed silent and returned to his desk to grab his suit coat before we headed out.

We snagged a yellow cab at the corner, and I rattled off the address of a steakhouse in midtown. Jamison Kennedy was waiting for us when we arrived. We'd met him in college, all three of us finance majors. After graduation, he'd worked as a stockbroker while my brother and I opened K-Corp, our investment banking firm. Eventually, Jamison had made a name for himself and started his own investment firm. His business boomed, and he ended up making his first billion a few years before us.

Recently, he'd approached us about merging our companies. Since Justice and I had already made a couple of offers over the years, we jumped at the chance. We'd even made the lame joke that it was perfect because Kennedy fit right in with K-Corp. But, what we didn't understand was why he'd finally agreed.

Jamison stood and shook our hands before we all took our seats. "You boys still planning on being at the wedding this weekend?" he asked after we'd placed our orders.

"What kind of groomsmen would we be if we skipped out?" I joked with a grin.

He eyed me darkly. "The kind who get their assess kicked all the way to Timbuck-fucking-tu if they're even a minute late. This day has to be perfect for my Hazel."

Justice took a sip of the scotch the waiter had just placed in front of him before reassuring Jamison. "As tempted as I am to be late just to see you try and kick my ass, we'll report as scheduled, boss."

Jamison nodded his thanks, and we started talking business. Justice was barely paying attention, throwing in one-word answers from time to time while he vigilantly checked his phone.

The plan Jamison laid out had him still running the division but stepping back considerably and relying on his VPs and managers. Knowing him as I did, I was well aware that he was as much of a workaholic as I was, so I voiced my curiosity. "What convinced you to lighten the load?"

"Hazel," he answered without hesitation. "I want to spend my life with her, not in my office with a scotch and a headache."

I laughed and nodded. "Fair enough." It made sense since I'd been ruminating on the idea of working less once I'd brought Imogene home. I didn't want to miss any time with her or our kids, and since I fully intended to put a baby in her without delay, it seemed like a good time to start the ball rolling.

Justice stood suddenly and excused himself before weaving through the tables and exiting the restaurant. The look on his face told me he wouldn't be returning. Jamison raised a brow in question, and I shrugged. "Probably something to do with a woman," I answered, being deliberately vague. The last thing any of us needed was someone over-hearing about Blair, digging up the info, and making a big deal out of it while we were trying to make a smooth merger. Alarming stock-holders would be a gigantic pain in the ass.

As expected, I got a text a couple of minutes later that something had come up and he wouldn't be back.

The business discussion with Jamison concluded shortly, and we spent a few more minutes catching up as we waited for the check. After we paid and walked out into the spring night, he made me promise once again to be on time for the wedding. Then we separated, and I headed home.

Chapter 2
THATCHER

My eyes swept over the half-finished room, and anger bubbled beneath the surface of my calm façade. If I ever saw my old contractor, I was going to shove my foot so far up his ass he'd be chewing leather for months. I pushed my violent daydreams aside and focused on the new guy who was surveying the space and looking over my list of requirements.

He finally wrote one last note on his clipboard and faced me. "We can definitely get it done, but to meet the time frame, we'll have to work around the clock."

I nodded. "Whatever it takes." I hardly slept these days anyway. I ached for my girl when I was in bed alone. If I did finally drift off, it was only to be woken up a little later drenched in sweat and crying out her name as I came like a fucking teenager. It was ridiculous. Thirty-four years old, and I was regularly having wet dreams.

I mentally sighed. I knew the only way to relieve this constant ache in my heart and balls was to get Imogene in our bed and sink ten inches deep into her dripping pussy. I could almost feel the slide of my cock between her lips. It showed just how talented my imagination was considering I'd never had my dick between a woman's legs. Or anywhere else on a woman's body.

For a long time, I'd thought I was simply broken. I'd even briefly wondered if I was batting for the wrong team. But there'd been no spark for either sex. I'd finally confided in Justice about it in my early twenties, and after a night spent with Patti and her family, he came to a conclusion that hadn't occurred to me.

"I've seen the way you watch Pattie and Don," he told me as we'd walked back to our office building. We were still at the stage where every penny was being poured back into the business, which meant we were on intimate terms with the couches in our offices. "I've also observed it with other couples." He stopped, and I halted next to him. He put a hand on my shoulder and looked me straight in the eye. "You want what they have. You long for it." He was right. Patti and Don had exactly what I was hoping to find someday. They adored each other. Whenever they were together, it was rare that they weren't touching in some way. I wanted a love like that. I knew I was capable of it, but I wanted my woman's love to be mine as much as mine was hers.

"Thatcher," he continued. "Your heart and body are telling you what your brain hasn't concluded yet. They won't work until you've found the right woman."

He'd been right, but I hadn't realized quite how accurate he actually was until the day I first saw Imogene. My heart had sped up and raced like it was in the Indy 500, and I'd had to step in front of a park bench to hide the hard on that was suddenly tenting my pants. I'd been sporting a semi ever since.

"Mr. Kendall?" The contractor pulled me back to the present, and I pushed away all of my other thoughts. He handed me the clipboard, and I quickly scrawled my signature before passing it back. "My crew will be here in a few hours to get started."

"Thanks," I said as I walked him down three flights of stairs to the front door. I had an elevator at the back of the house, but I rarely used it. It was going to come in very handy when Imogene was pregnant, though.

The contractor and I shook hands, and then he was gone. The renovations were on the fourth floor, so I wandered back to the master suite on the second floor, intending to gather some stuff and sleep in the finished basement so I wouldn't be too disturbed by the noise.

Instead, my bare feet padded along the shiny, hardwood floors until I was standing in the doorway to the room just across the hall. It had been finished only a few weeks after I'd started the renovations on my brownstone. The changes had been simpler, and I wasn't adding a sunroom onto it like I was on the fourth floor.

The walls were painted a soft yellow, a big picture window looked out over the street, and it was flanked by two white, built-in bookcases. On the left end of the wall, in the corner, was a cream and wood glider with a teddy bear already propped in the seat, ready for some cuddling. The next wall had a white crib and changing table, as well as other necessary items for a nursery. The opposite corner of the room had a little nook with cupboards waiting to be filled with toys, and the wall beside it was taken up by a white chest of drawers and the door to a walk-in closet. Everything was neutral so it would work for a girl or a boy, but I had done it more so that everything could be easily changed based on what Imogene wanted.

Staring at the nursery I'd had built for the babies I planned to have with her; I made a decision. Whether her other surprise was ready or not, I was bringing my woman home in two weeks.

"IMOGENE," I groaned as I pumped my hips in a steady rhythm. Her legs wrapped around me, and she arched her back, shoving her sweet tits in my face. They were perfect, like two scoops of vanilla ice cream with red cherries on top. They were going to be even more mouthwatering when they were dripping with milk. I bent my head to suck one tight peak into my mouth, sucking hard, as though I could already drink from her.

My spine started tingling, and I lifted my head to grit my teeth as I pushed back my pending orgasm. I switched to her other breast, and Imogene clutched my biceps, her nails digging into my skin as she cried out in ecstasy. They were going to leave marks, and it made the caveman inside me roar with approval. I wanted her to brand me as hers, just as the love bites around her tits and the bruises she would no doubt sport on her hips from my firm grip marked her as mine.

I popped her nipple from my mouth and kissed the valley

between her tits before demanding, "Tell me you love me, sugar." I needed to hear it. There was no stronger aphrodisiac than hearing my woman profess her love. I was completely obsessed with Imogene, and I wanted—no, needed—her to feel the same way.

Her eyes met mine, and they were brimming with emotion. "I love you so much, Thatcher."

It was all I needed. I reached between us and pinched her clit just before I thrust in one last time, burying myself as deep as possible and coming with a shout. The second I started to release inside her, Imogene exploded, her head dropping back as she screamed my name.

I rocked against her, prolonging our orgasms as long as possible. Eventually, we lay there, limp and utterly spent. I stayed inside her, plugging her hole so no come would leak out of her. My boys were on a mission, and I was doing everything I could to help them out. After a while, I grew tired from holding myself up so that I wouldn't squish her petite body beneath my massive one. I fucking loved the way I could cover her from head to toe, though.

Rolling to the side, I sighed in contentment as I cuddled Imogene against me. I kissed the top of her head and lifted her face, her lips searching for mine. I obliged her silent request, kissing her passionately. The taste of cinnamon and sugar burst on my tongue as it tangled with hers.

My eyes opened, and I stared at the empty spot beside me on the bed. My body was sweating and shaking from the force of my orgasm, but as my hand slid over the soft sheets, feeling their coolness, the chill spread from my fingertips to the rest of me. These dreams left me feeling bereft and alone. The funny thing was, despite coming during the dream, it wasn't the ejaculation that had my dick going limp when I woke up. It was remembering that I was alone, and it was always a long time before I fell into another restless sleep.

Chapter 3
THATCHER

Hazel and Jamison were like magnets, neither of them could be far from the other for long. It was clear how much they adored each other, and Jamison made no attempt to hide the fact that he worshipped her.

They'd had a big, beautiful wedding ceremony at St. Patrick's Cathedral, which I still believe Jamison had to perform a hit for someone in order to get it on a month's notice. That or he had a direct line to God, and they personally made a deal.

Their reception was at the Plaza and required all guests to attend in black tie. The whole event was full of glitz and glitter. The guest list was littered with New York's elite.

It was incredible, but not my scene. I was pretty sure it wasn't Jamison's either, so it must've all been for Hazel. And yet, whenever I spotted her, unless she was looking at Jamison, her eyes lost some of their sparkle and she seemed almost uncomfortable in her own skin.

Justice had ducked out early; to go home and brood over Blair, no doubt. I had intended to do the same, but my house was full of people and incredibly lonely at the same time.

After saying goodbye to the bride and groom, I found myself taking the green line down to South Ferry. It was a warm evening, so I removed my tux jacket and folded it over my arm. Then I wandered along the park towards the bench where I stopped every day and watched Imogene.

To my surprise, there was someone already sitting there. I hesitated, preferring to be alone with my misery, but a niggling feeling kept my feet moving. My heart started pounding, beating faster the closer I got. When I was only a few feet away, the person lifted her head and warm, whiskey-colored eyes locked with mine. My breath stuck in my throat as I stood there like a deer caught in headlights.

It was the first time Imogene and I had ever come face to face. She was even more beautiful up close, and I continued to struggle to breathe. My body had gone on high alert, spreading goosebumps over my skin, and my dick sprung to attention.

My eyes finally broke from hers to take in the rest of Imogene. She was sitting cross-legged on the bench, a sketchbook in her lap and a pencil in her hand. She was wearing a baggy sweatshirt that came to her knees and dipped off one shoulder. Despite the shapelessness, it didn't disguise her long, lithe body, particularly with her legs in legging type pants that hugged her like a second skin. They must have been a light brown or peach color because in the dark, with only the moon and street lamps illuminating the area, her legs looked bare.

I frowned and glared at the leggings. Any red-blooded man would take one look at those and picture them wrapped around his waist. Yeah. That shit wasn't going to fly with me. Those were going right in the trash once I got her home. *Their days were numbered.*

"Pardon?" Her voice was low and husky, washing over me, leaving my nerve endings tingling. When I lifted my eyes to her face, she was watching me expectantly. It took me a beat, but then I realized I must have said that last thought out loud.

"Nothing, beautiful," I told her with a small shake of my head.

She cocked her head to the side, and her shoulder-length, light brown curls bounced. "Um, okay." Her face was scrubbed free of makeup, and pink lips were flanked by dimples that I itched to explore with my tongue. She looked so young and innocent. I'd even wondered that maybe I was dooming myself to my brother's shoes. Not that it would have altered my course of action. Just delayed things a bit. But once I had her name, I quickly discovered that she was nineteen; to my cock's utter relief. The last two months had been sheer hell. I had no idea how my brother had held out for two years. Maybe it should have given me pause that I was fifteen years older than her, but I didn't give a fuck. She was mine.

There wasn't much more information on her. No address or phone number. She had no social media presence, and the only mention I found of her name was the obituary of an Imogene Delaney from Queens who'd died a few months ago. I'd hired a private investigator, but since there wasn't anything he could tell me that would change my mind about Imogene, I let him go after he gave me the basics about her.

I took a step closer, and she shut her sketch pad, holding it close to her chest. "May I sit?" I asked softly. I didn't want to spook her and send her running—not now that I finally had her attention.

She nodded, and I lowered my big frame onto the small bench. I took up most of the space, so she scooted over to make a little more room for me.

"My name is Thatcher." I smiled warmly, and she hesitantly returned the gesture. She looked nervous, but there was no fear in her eyes. Was she as comfortable with me as I was with her? Did she feel what was between us? She had to. There was no fucking way this was one-sided.

"Imogene," she responded. I kept the fact that I already knew her name to myself.

"Beautiful name for a beautiful girl." Even in the dim lighting, I was able to see the sprinkling of pink on her cheeks as she blushed.

I forced myself to tear my eyes away from her for a few minutes. My feelings for her were so intense that I wanted to ease her in, make her fall for me before she discovered the true depths of my obsession with her. That's when I noticed the portfolio propped on the seat next to her. I gestured to it and asked, "Will you show me some of your work? I've seen your displays, but I've never studied them up close. From what I can tell, you're incredibly talented."

Imogene's expression turned shy even as she beamed at me, lighting up the night more than the moon or stars ever could. She set her notebook on the bench between us and twisted to pick up her big, black folder.

A soft breeze blew in off the bay and fluttered the flimsy cover of the sketch pad. Imogene was just straightening up with a few papers in her hands when another, stronger wind blew the notebook open completely. She gasped, and my eyes locked on the detailed pencil drawing on the paper. It was me.

Imogene dropped the other pieces of art, and they slid to the ground as she scrambled to grab the sketch pad. I snatched it up before she could get to it and quickly thumbed through the pages. They were filled with drawings in pencil, charcoal, or oil pastels. There were also oil paintings and watercolors. There had to have been over sixty pictures, and they all had one thing in common. *Me*.

The realization that she couldn't stop thinking of me, to the point where she'd drawn my likeness dozens and dozens of times, had my heart throwing a fucking party in my chest. My dick was also eager to join the celebration, and I had to hold the pad over my lap while adjusting myself.

"Please give that back, Thatcher," she pleaded. I lifted my gaze and was startled by the distress on her face. Her whiskey eyes were churning with anxiety and fear. "I'm sorry. You just have such a beautiful face." Her hands moved wildly, gesturing as she rambled. "I swear, I'm not a crazy stalker." I almost burst into laughter at that but succeeded in muffling it and disguising it with a cough. She had no idea what a crazy stalker looked like.

That thought was like a splash of cold water, and the reality of where we were and what time it was suddenly sunk in. "Are you out of your mind?" I barked. Imogene reared back in shock, and I immediately regretted my tone. But all of the worst-case scenarios of a young woman in a park at night were playing out in my head, and the fear of what could have happened to her was manifesting itself in a ball of rage.

Imogene quickly seized the notebook from my hands and shoved it in her portfolio. Her feet brushed the fallen papers when she leaned over, and I bent down to pick them up for her. That's when I spotted the beat-up duffle bag tucked in underneath the bench.

I closed my eyes and tried to breathe steadily. That couldn't be what I thought it was, right? No way had I missed this. I opened my eyes again and stared at the bag. I didn't want to believe it, but I knew it was true. All that anger did a one-eighty and was fully unleashed on myself.

I'd spent the last two months preparing the

perfect home for Imogene, and during all that time she'd been living out of a duffle bag on the New York City streets.

"Fuck!" I growled harshly. I was going to fucking kill the PI I'd hired to dig into her. It never occurred to the asshole that she didn't have an address because she was fucking homeless? I cursed again as I grabbed the bag and shot to my feet, then quickly shoved the rest of the papers into her folder before taking that in the same hand as her bag. I used my unoccupied hand to take hers in a firm grip. Not hard enough to cause her pain but one I knew she couldn't escape from without a lot of effort. "Let's go," I gritted out as I stomped across the grass and bike path until I reached the street.

I contemplated texting my driver, but he would take too long, and since he was also my bodyguard and I'd slipped out on him, he was probably pissed as fuck. I didn't want to deal with his shit on top of everything with Imogene. Luck was on my side however, because a cab with a lit vacant sign turned the corner right as we reached the curb. I raised our joint hands in the air to flag him down. When I couldn't extend my arm the whole distance, I glanced down at Imogene and it dawned on me how small she was in comparison to me. She was slender and lean, which made her appear taller until she was next to a behemoth like me.

My brain could only handle so much as I thought about how her little body would feel cradled against mine. Or pressed beneath it. All the emotions churning inside me brought months of pent up desire to the surface. I licked my lips, and my eyes swept over her sexy little body.

My pants were bursting at the seams as my shaft fought the confines of my zipper. It was like my head had passed a note to my cock and gave it a heads up (pun intended) that we would soon be near a bed.

The cab screeched to a stop in front of us, and I took a deep breath, willing my dick to back the fuck off. I turned and guided Imogene to the back of the cab. As I helped her in, I noticed her downturned head and the slump of her shoulders.

Shit. I knew I needed to smooth things over with her, but I had to get control of myself first.

I gave the driver my address and put the cab number into an app to pay automatically. Then I shot off a quick text to my contractor, instructing them to clear out of the house for the next few days, but continue to bill me. After putting it back in my pocket, I glanced at Imogene just as she turned watery eyes in my direction. "I'm really sorry,

Thatcher. Where are you taking me? Please let me go. If I promise not to come anywhere near you from now on, can we just forget this ever happened?" she pleaded.

Forget? That wasn't possible. There wasn't one thing about Imogene that wasn't burned into my mind. She shifted so she was facing me and put her unoccupied hand on my thigh. I stiffened and sucked in a deep breath. My skin burned underneath her touch, and all I wanted was to feel that heat on every inch of me.

"Don't," I said through clenched teeth. "I am hanging on by a thread. If you touch me, I'm going to fucking lose it."

Chapter 4
THATCHER

Imogene's hand flew back like she'd been burned, which was fitting since my leg felt like it had been singed where she'd touched it. Then she scooted to the far edge of the seat and curled into herself.

The cab driver was tossing suspicious glances at us, and I knew I needed to diffuse the situation quickly. Even though it was unlikely that he could hear anything we were saying, Imogene's body language was probably sending up alarms.

I expelled a slow breath and pictured Imogene painting in our home. It was soothing and helped to ease my tension.

"Imogene," I said softly as I reached out to draw my fingertips down her cheek. I wasn't sure how I'd expected her to react, but I was elated when she instinctively leaned into my touch. "I'm taking you home, sugar."

Her brows drew down, and her eyes darkened to amber as confusion floated across her face. "I don't have a home."

Her words caused an ache in my chest, but I reminded myself that it was all about to get better. "Yes, you do."

Imogene shook her head in denial. "No. I mean, I did. But then my grandmother died, and they wouldn't let me stay in her apartment in Queens"—a piece of the puzzle slid into place. Imogene Delaney must have been her grandmother—"and I don't have a home now."

"You do," I insisted. "I'm going to make sure you don't spend one more fucking night on the streets. You're coming home with me, sugar." And sleeping in our bed. But we'd get into that later.

Imogene gasped, gaping at me with disbelief. "I don't even know you!"

I speared her with an intense stare. "Yes, you do. I know you feel what's between us, Imogene. You may not have realized it, but you know me."

Her expression turned less fierce, and there wasn't much conviction in her tone when she said, "I don't know what you mean."

If I hadn't seen her sketches of me, I might've

had a moment of doubt. But I had, and they'd reinforced my certainty that we were meant to be together. Before she knew what was happening, I'd picked her up and put her on my lap so that she was straddling my legs. "I'll prove it," I growled before I cupped her face in my hands and crashed my mouth down over hers.

Imogene stiffened for a half of a second but when the tip of my tongue traced her bottom lip, she sighed and melted right into me. Her exhalation gave me the opening I needed to slide my tongue into her mouth. My body sizzled with need and excitement as I tangled my tongue with hers. My hands delved into her silky curls, and I slanted her head to deepen the angle of the kiss.

She tasted sweet, like cinnamon and sugar, and I was suddenly ravenously hungry. I was on the verge of taking it too far, especially since we were in the back of a taxi. So, I pulled back and pressed her head into my chest, my hands slipping down to rub her back gently. We were both panting, and I could feel her heart racing. "I think I made my point," I murmured. She made an unintelligible sound, which I chose to take as an affirmative.

My hands rubbed soft circles on her back when I found the courage to voice a question I'd dreaded. I was pretty sure I knew the answer, and it wouldn't change how I felt about her, but it might lead me to kill someone. "Are you untouched, sugar?"

"Mmmhmm." She barely acknowledged my question, but it was all I needed. A huge fucking weight lifted from my shoulders.

By the time the car came to a stop, our breathing had evened out, and Imogene was relaxed and snuggled up against me. Not a great situation for trying to keep my cock calm, but I'd never turn down the chance to have her in my arms.

The driver turned around as far as he could in his seat and glared at me. Then he glanced at Imogene. "You okay, lady? Want me to call the cops?"

I rolled my eyes and glanced down at Imogene's slumped body. I almost laughed when I realized she was fast asleep, but I didn't want to wake her. She looked so peaceful and completely exhausted. Clearly, her body knew she was safe with me. Her head would catch up soon enough. But what I wanted most was her heart. I wanted her love.

"She's fine," I told the cabbie, my tone and expression making it very clear that he should mind his own damn business. He huffed but flipped around and faced the front without another word.

I put one hand on her ass while the other stayed

on her back to keep her secure. Then I carefully slid over the bench seat, trying not to jostle her too much. I extended my hand and just barely managed to pull the handle on the door and use my foot to push it open. It took a little creative maneuvering, but I managed to get out of the taxi and to my feet without waking Imogene. She wrapped herself around me and clung like a little monkey, which allowed me to grab her duffel—with her folder already stuffed inside—too.

After dropping her stuff just inside the doorway, getting her into the house and up to the bedroom was much easier. I didn't bother with the light as I padded across the carpet to the huge bed on the opposite wall. Once I'd drawn down the covers and laid Imogene on the bed, I contemplated my next move. The clothes she was wearing didn't look terribly uncomfortable, but I was positive she'd sleep better in something else. I also didn't hate the idea of her sleeping in something of mine.

As quietly as possible, I walked to a long, walnut dresser that sat on the next wall by the door of the large walk-in closet. I slid open the second drawer down on the left and rooted through it until I found what I was looking for. Then I returned to the bed and thought about the files of my most boring clients the whole time I changed her out of her clothes, discarding her leggings and underwear in the trash bin in the bathroom, and dressed her in an old t-shirt from my college football days. It had my name on the back in bold, black letters, which made me grin as I gathered the rest of her clothes and went into the closet.

The townhouse was over a hundred years old and had been on the verge of being condemned when I bought it. I restored as much as possible and gutted the rest. One of the features that remained was a laundry shoot on each floor. On this level, it was located in the master bedroom's walk-in. I dropped Imogene's garments into the shoot, then stripped and did the same with mine. I hesitated when I reached for the waistband of my boxers. Generally, I slept naked and didn't plan on changing that just because Imogene was in my bed. However, I also didn't want to overwhelm her too much when she woke up beside me our first morning together. So, I kept them on and made a quick trip to the bathroom before crawling into bed. I tugged the soft blue, down comforter up and over us. Imogene sighed and immediately rolled towards me, plastering her body against mine.

She felt so fucking good. I wrapped my arms

around her and inhaled deeply, scenting cinnamon and sugar again. This was what I'd been waiting for. This was what my future held. She didn't realize it yet, but when she fell asleep on me, she had chosen to be mine.

Chapter 5
THATCHER

My eyes opened, and I stared through the relative darkness in my room. There was a storm raging outside, and it hid the morning sun. There was just enough light for me to see that I was either deeply immersed in another dream, or life had finally taken the turn I'd been working towards.

For the first time in my life, I wasn't alone when I woke in the morning. The most beautiful woman I'd ever laid eyes on was curled up in my embrace. I was spooning her small body, and her sweet little ass was wreaking havoc on my morning wood.

Imogene sighed and wiggled back a little farther into me, making me grunt and mutter, "fuck." Every muscle in her body tensed; she even stopped breathing.

I dipped my head and nibbled on her ear, grinning when she blew out a breath and shivered. "Good morning," I murmured.

"Um, Thatcher?"

"Hmmm, hearing my name in your raspy morning voice is sexy as hell, baby." I kissed her neck, and my tongue darted out to taste her skin. A groan escaped my lips at the subtle flavor of cinnamon and sugar. I was convinced she was going to taste that sweet everywhere.

I gently tugged on her ear lobe with my teeth, then let it go as I scooted a few inches away so I could roll her onto her back. Her whiskey orbs were staring up at me with confusion, but there was also a spark of desire.

Quickly, I shifted so I was hovering over her, blanketing her entire body. I pushed her hair away from her neck, and my lips found purchase on the soft skin there. "You taste so fucking delectable," I muttered before sucking lightly.

"I—uh—thought you were mad," she stammered, even as she tilted her head to give me better access. "I figured you were taking me to get a restraining order or something."

I chuckled and raised my head to look her in the eye. "No, sugar. Pretty much the exact opposite."

"What?" she asked breathily, though she watched me warily.

"Now that I know about your obsession with me"—she blushed furiously and tried to break our eye contact. It was adorable, but I grasped her chin to keep our gazes locked—"I'm going to keep you as close as possible."

"I don't understand. You're keeping me prisoner? I swear, I'm not a fanatical stalker or anything. You just have such a beautiful face, the artist in me couldn't help capturing it on paper. You don't have to—" She stopped rambling when I threw my head back and belly laughed. Damn, she was fucking cute.

"As appealing as the idea is, I'm not going to keep you prisoner, Imogene."

"But you said—" I cut her off by placing my index finger over her pink lips.

"You have no idea what obsessed truly looks like, sugar," I told her seriously. "I knew you were mine the moment I saw you for the first time. And, I've been preparing for you ever since. I wanted everything to be perfect so you would come willingly and never want to leave my side." I shook my head ruefully and grimaced. "If I had known you were sleeping on the streets, I would have said fuck it and brought you home sooner." I was going to be kicking my own ass over that for a long time.

"I didn't think you'd ever noticed me," Imogene

responded with wide eyes, still confused but also curious. And perhaps it was wishful thinking on my part, but it looked like there was hope lurking in her amber depths.

"I more than noticed you, sugar. I claimed you."

Her mouth dropped open and while I was tempted to take the opportunity to kiss her again, I knew once I started, I wouldn't be able to stop. "Let me show you," I whispered. Half-heartedly, I left the warmth of her body and climbed from the bed.

Imogene paled when she saw my almost naked body. Her eyes devoured me with a hunger that made me swell and harden even more than I had been from lying on top of her.

My big cock tented my boxers, and the movement drew her attention. Once again, her jaw dropped, and her cheeks turned bright red. She licked her lips, and I clenched my hands into fists and grunted, "Sugar, if you don't stop looking at me like that, I'm going to give that hungry mouth something to suck on. And, that would be a waste of my come." I didn't think she could blush any harder, but I'd obviously been wrong.

"Why?" she squeaked. I wasn't ready to explain, so I just shook my head and held out my hand.

"Let me show you something."

Imogene slowly put her delicate hand in mine,

and I engulfed it in my own as I helped her off the bed. She glanced down at her outfit and gasped. "Wh—where are my clothes? How did I get undressed? I'm not wearing any freaking underwear! Whose—"

I'd had enough of the wait and stopped the stream of words by yanking her into my arms and kissing the fuck out of her. She melted into me like I knew she would, her mouth opening to give me access. Her velvety tongue slid along mine as she tentatively kissed me back. I sighed and used every ounce of my self-control to pull back.

"Don't worry about your old clothes. I undressed you. Hell yes, I looked my fill. But no, I didn't give in to the desire to cop a feel. You're wearing my shirt because I needed to know I was as close to you as possible, even if it was just my clothes,"—I turned her so that our sides were facing a tall mirror standing in the corner by the dresser. Then I angled her a little more so she could see the back. "And, I fucking love seeing you marked with my name."

Before she could ask any more questions, I took her hand again and led her downstairs to the kitchen. Imogene was silent, her eyes bouncing around, taking in everything around her. I sat her at the island and made her some toast—with cinnamon and sugar of course—and orange juice.

"You're going to need your strength," I told her as I slid the food in front of her. She looked as though she wanted to ask more questions, but I just shook my head and lifted the bread to her mouth. "I promise to answer all of your questions soon, sugar. Eat first."

She narrowed her eyes suspiciously but chomped down, taking a big bite of her snack. A little moan of delight slipped from between her lips, and I had to turn away and take several deep breaths while running baseball stats in my head to keep from throwing her down on the island and taking her right then.

When I felt a little more stable, I turned back around to see she was just finishing her toast. I scooted her untouched orange juice towards her. "Drink. The vitamins are good for you." I didn't know how malnourished she was from living on the streets, but I'd also read that the vitamins in orange juice were good for pregnant women.

I was satisfied to see her drain the glass without argument. "Good girl," I praised her softly before taking her glass and dish to the sink. Then I returned to her side and laced our fingers together. I guided her on a short tour of the house, and she continued to take it all in with awe. Every time her lips tipped up, I felt a zing of happiness that she was pleased with our home. If she didn't like it, I would have moved in a heartbeat, but it seemed that wouldn't be necessary.

Finally, we ended up at the closed door across from the master bedroom. We'd seen everything else except the fourth floor, which I was saving for later.

I positioned Imogene in front of me, her back to my front. I put one hand on her currently flat stomach and used the other to pull her hair to one side so I could kiss her neck. When she shivered, it confirmed what I'd been starting to realize; this was a sensitive spot for her. I filed that information away for future use.

"I told you I've been preparing for you since the moment I saw you," I whispered in her ear. Imogene nodded, causing her head to bump mine and making me chuckle. Keeping her snug against me, I moved my free hand to the silver handle on the door. "Not just you, sugar," I informed her as I nudged it open. "I've been getting ready for our family."

Imogene gasped when the door swung open fully and she got her first look at the nursery. I nudged her forward but kept her locked in my embrace, so we stepped in together. "Do you like it?"

Her eyes swept from side to side, and she sighed, "It's gorgeous." Her head twisted and tipped back so she could look up at me. "Our family?" she asked softly.

I nodded and tipped my face down to brush a tender kiss across her lips. The hand on her stomach fisted the fabric, and I glided the other up her thigh and under the hem of my shirt to cup her pussy. "I'm going to put a baby in your belly as soon as I pop this sweet cherry, sugar. I intend to fill this room as many times as you'll let me." Her pussy was already slippery and wet but as I spoke, she soaked my fingers.

I slid them between her drenched folds, and Imogene moaned as her eyelids drifted shut. Then I brought them to my mouth and sucked them clean. "Fuck, I knew you'd taste like cinnamon and sugar here too."

My dick was poking insistently into her round, little ass, leaking come from the painfully tight head. My hand returned to between her legs, and I cupped her again, dipping my middle finger in to penetrate her this time. I moved it in and out a few times, making sure to circle her sensitive bud each time. "Ohhh," Imogene moaned. Fuck, if she made this much noise from a little finger fucking, I couldn't wait to hear her when she was riding my dick.

I sped up my fingers, adding another and then carefully working in a third before she began to shake uncontrollably. "Hold on to me, sugar." Dutifully, her hands raised and wound around my neck. I kept her secure with my arm around her waist, holding her up when her legs became unsteady. Her reaction was so raw. When her eyes flew to mine, she even looked a little scared of what was happening. "Have you ever had an orgasm, Imogene?" She shook her head frantically and fuck, being the first and only man to give her that pleasure had the beast inside me roaring with approval. "I've got you. Trust me to take care of you and just let go." The nervousness dissipated a little, and she swallowed hard before she visibly relaxed. On the next pass over her clit, I stopped my hand and pinched the hard nub before plunging my fingers back inside her. Imogene cried out as her orgasm washed over her. She shuddered in waves, and her pelvis shamelessly rocked into my hand. It was the most beautiful thing I'd ever seen, and I fucking lost it.

Chapter 6
THATCHER

"I need to be inside you," I growled as I flipped her around and lowered her to the thick, plush carpet. In the recesses of my mind, it registered that we were only a few feet from our bed, but I couldn't manage to convince myself to wait. Besides, it seemed fitting to make our first baby in the nursery.

I whipped the shirt over her head and kicked off my boxers before straddling her legs and looking my fill. Her body was slender, but it still curved in all the right places and something whispered to me that she was ripe and ready for me to breed her. The neatly trimmed, light-brown thatch of curls between her legs glistened, and I licked my lips, already tasting her sweetness on my tongue.

Her eyed were riveted to my hard on, and she

looked freaked out. "You're huge," she whispered, her voice trembling with trepidation.

I couldn't deny that I was well endowed, and I could understand why she was worried since she was so tiny compared to me. But I had no doubts about our compatibility. I cupped her cheek and waited until she met my gaze. "We were made for each other. We'll fit perfectly. Trust me." She glanced down again but then nodded.

"You are so fucking gorgeous," I grunted as I began to explore her with the palms of my hands. When I reached her tits, I cupped them and leaned down to lick each cherry tip. "These are perfect but fuck, sugar. Just the thought of them big and swollen with milk has me on the verge of blowing my load all over you. And, I intend to be buried deep in your womb before that happens."

As I licked around her nipples some more, I glanced up at her and saw her looking at me with wide, whiskey eyes. They were cloudy with passion but also churning with a variety of other emotions.

"Don't be scared, sugar," I soothed as I leaned up to kiss her softly. "I know you feel this between us. Don't fight it." Pulling back a few inches, I stared into her face. "You want this, Imogene. Don't you? I can see it in your eyes." She hesitated for a moment, then nodded with a timid smile. I gently kneaded her tits as I kissed her to let her know I was pleased with her answer.

After a few minutes, I tore my lips away and leaned over to snatch a small pillow off of the rocker; then I shoved it under her hips. I watched her steadily as I moved into place, and the tip of my cock nudged her entrance. A thought filtered through my head, and I narrowed my eyes at her. "You're not on birth control, are you?" She shook her head, and I exhaled in relief. "I'm not pulling out, sugar," I stated with determination. "I'm going to fill your unprotected womb so full that there will be no way in hell you don't end up pregnant." I pressed the head in so just the tip was bathed in her heat and groaned, "Fuck."

Imogene moaned and her walls spasmed, encouraging me to push in until I felt resistance. I hesitated for a moment, frustrated that I had no choice but to cause her pain. "I'm sorry, sugar." I kissed her with all the passion inside me while I plucked and twisted her nipples until she was whimpering and squirming, trying to get more of my dick inside her. Then I grabbed her hips and plunged in, popping her cherry and burying myself to the root. "Oh, fuck!" I shouted. She was like a fucking vice as she clamped down around me. Though it strained every muscle in my body, I managed to stay still as she stretched and adjusted to my size. A few tears tracked from the corners of her eyes, and I bent to kiss them away.

After a minute, her expression began to clear of any lingering pain, and I shifted experimentally. Imogene's head thumped back on the carpet when she threw it back and cried out.

"Holy crap," she exclaimed in a loud whisper. "That was—holy crap."

I grinned and this time, I pulled out a few inches before gliding back in. "Yesss!" she hissed. "Don't stop!" I repeated the motion, and she yelled as her hands delved into her hair, clutching the strands like a life line. "Please, Thatcher," she whimpered, arching beneath me.

Hearing my name was like lighting a match and throwing it on gasoline. I grabbed her thighs and put her legs around my waist before palming her ass and yanking her down on my cock as I surged inside her over and over. I retreated almost all the way, then slammed back in until I nudged her cervix.

My spine started to tingle, and I clenched my ass in an effort to keep from coming as my hips bucked wildly. But Imogene's untried pussy was so hot and tight, I was quickly losing all control.

"Thatcher," she moaned as she writhed beneath me.

Fuck. Fuck. Fuck. If she kept saying my name like that, I was going to blow before I could make her come. And, I needed her to come first so her body would be soft and open, ready to take every drop of my seed.

"Damn, baby," I groaned. "You feel so fucking good." I'd never imagined sex would feel this incredible, but something told me it would only have ever been like this with Imogene. It made me even happier that I'd waited for her. The knowledge that I was breaching her virgin pussy with my own untouched cock—knowing we were each other's first and only—it was like a drug.

I was losing the fight to keep myself in check and decided to push the boundaries with a little dirty talk and see how she responded. "You're doing so good, sugar," I praised her with a grunt as I pounded even harder. "Your little pussy is so snug, I can barely get my dick out. I think you like having my giant cock in your tight hole. Oh, fuck. Yes!" Imogene's inner walls clenched, and she cried out. She was getting noisier, and it was hot as hell. I leaned up and stared at where we were connected, watching myself disappear inside her and come out again coated in her cream. "I'm going to break you in eventually, sugar. You'll be able to spread your legs and take me whenever and wherever I need you."

"Yes! Thatcher! Yes!"

"I bet you'll be the one begging for it once you're bred though, won't you?" I bowed down and licked around one of her nipples before giving it a little bite. "You have no idea how fucking hot it makes me to picture you round and swollen with our baby. Your hips lush and wide, your tits big and aching for my touch."

I was pushing myself over the fucking edge, so it was a damn good thing I'd worked her up too. "Tilt that pussy, sugar," I growled. "Open wide and take me deep. I want you to milk my cock of every drop. We're going to get you good and knocked up on the first fucking try. Fuck! Fuck! That's it, sugar. Yes!"

Imogene went off like a rocket, soaring high and exploding with an ear-piercing scream. I followed right behind as her pussy massaged my dick. Hot streams of come gushed from my shaft, filling her so full it oozed out. The sticky mixture of us created a slippery passage for me to slide in even deeper.

"Thatcher," Imogene moaned as I continued to

pump an endless stream of hot liquid. "More," she begged as her walls clamped tight around me. With each spurt, she moaned and pleaded for me to move harder and faster. *Holy shit.* She was getting off on the fact that I was coming inside her.

If I hadn't already known she was the perfect woman for me, that would have convinced me. Since my dick hadn't softened in the least, I gave her exactly what she asked for. I fucked her long and hard until we'd both come again, and again.

She was going to be sore as fuck the next day, but I'd never be able to deny her anything. It wasn't until we were so exhausted that we couldn't move that we finally stopped. I dropped down beside Imogene on the carpet, keeping an arm and leg thrown over her. She laid her head on my outstretched arm, and I cupped her pussy, my hand trying it's best to keep my come inside her.

I woke up a few hours later and had just enough energy to stand and lift Imogene into my arms. After stumbling across the hall, I gently set her down on the bed, then crawled in and wrapped myself around her before passing out again.

"THATCHER?"

Imogene's sweet voice penetrated my sleep, and I lazily opened my eyes. She was sitting up in bed with the covers around her waist, baring her gorgeous tits. Her hair was in crazy curls, her lips kiss-swollen, and she looked a little dazed and confused. I couldn't help the satisfied smile that crept over my face while I stared at my beautiful girl. She was finally mine. For the first time in months, I could breathe easy.

I dragged her down into my embrace. "Yes, sugar?"

"So, I wasn't dreaming?"

I laughed and kissed her on the nose. "Nothing could be more real."

Imogene's eyes studied me intently, full of questions. I sat up and scooted back until I was leaning against the headboard. Then I easily lifted her body and sat her on my lap, her legs straddling my hips. It brought our centers flush against each other, but I ignored the draining of my blood to my cock and focused on my woman. "What's going on in that mind of yours?"

She glanced down and picked nervously at her nails until I stilled her hands by wrapping them in mine. "Everything you're saying sounds like a dream."

"Good," I answered with a firm nod. "I want to make your every dream come true, Imogene."

"But"—she raised her eyes to meet mine, and her expression was earnest—"how do you know I'm really what you want? Forever? Why didn't you feel this way with any of the other women you've been with?"

My eyebrows shot to my hairline as I gaped at her for half a second. *Other what?* In the next second, I mentally slapped myself upside the head for being such an idiot. I placed a palm on each of her cheeks and tenderly cradled her face. Her small hands wrapped around my wrists, and her eyes closed as she leaned into my touch. "Imogene"—her lids lifted and her whiskey eyes glued to mine—"I've loved you since the moment I saw you. I've never felt anything like this for someone else"—her eyes widened—"Even before I knew you, I loved the idea of you. So, I waited. For you."

She tilted her head to the side, her expression confused. "Waited?"

"Sugar, I've never been with another woman. I was waiting for the love of my life."

Her mouth went slack, her jaw dropping a little and her lips forming a little O. "I didn't build that nursery for just anyone. I built this whole house for you. *You."* I brushed my lips over her cheeks and then mouth before saying, "Let me prove it to you."

Her eyes lit up, and she rocked against me. I laughed even as I groaned. "Not like that, sugar. As much as I want you, you're already going to be sore today." I frowned. "I never should have taken you so roughly your first time," I sighed "I seem to lose all sense when I'm around you."

Imogene smiled shyly, but it turned sly when she rocked against me a little more insistently. I scowled and quickly set her away from me. "You're going to earn yourself a spanking, sugar." She pouted, and it made me laugh again before I kissed her nose.

I got out of bed, then helped her climb out and get to her feet. Then I grabbed another shirt and slipped it over her too-tempting body before throwing on a pair of low-hanging sweatpants.

We made our way down the hall to the elevator at the back of the townhouse. She gawked at the contraption, and I chuckled as we stepped inside. I pressed the button for the fourth floor. "It's only two flights, why are we taking the elevator?" she asked.

"I wanted to show you where it was. I promise, if you took the stairs right now, you'd realize just how sore you are." She rolled her eyes, and I speared her with a direct, unyielding stare. "I expect you to use this when you're pregnant, Imogene. I don't care if it's only one flight."

"Thatch—"

"This isn't a discussion, sugar," I interrupted with a firm tone. "I won't chance anything happening to you and our baby."

A tinge of desperation bled through my words, and her expression softened as she agreed, "Okay."

Just then, the car came to a stop and opened into the room I'd been waiting on. "I wanted this to be done before I brought you home," I confessed quietly as she walked into the room.

I'd built her a studio. A big, open room with a lot of windows and natural light. But I'd also had a wall knocked down to create a small room with walls of glass, with French doors connecting it to the rest of the room, that the construction crew was still working on.

The studio was stocked with everything the owner of the art store had told me it needed. I was sure there were things he'd insisted on that were unnecessary, but I'd bought everything, just in case. I wanted Imogene to have anything and everything she desired.

"I can't believe you did this for me," she breathed as she did a slow turn in the center of the room.

I went to her and pulled her into my arms. "Haven't you realized it yet, sugar? I'd do anything for you."

Imogene beamed at me, then ducked her head as her smile turned shy. "And you want a baby momma in return?" Her tone was teasing, but I heard the undercurrent in her tone, afraid I would confirm what she feared.

"If your definition of baby momma means my wife, lover, and the mother of my children, then sure," I replied dryly. "But really, those are just perks since there's really only one thing I want."

She looked up at me, a smile playing at the corners of her lips. "What's the one thing?"

"Your love." Being so honest made me terrifyingly vulnerable, but I didn't want to play games.

Imogene suddenly threw herself into my arms. "You've had my love since the moment I first drew your picture," she admitted in my ear as she squeezed the air out of my chest.

I cough-laughed as I loosened her arms and dragged in some oxygen. My face must have expressed the level of my joy because she smiled so brightly that it rivaled the sun. I was sure it would cause the storm outside to clear any minute.

"I used to dream that you would notice me, and we would have a fairy-tale, happily ever after. But I thought it was a stupid fantasy, I never thought it could really happen. And yet, I couldn't stop myself from falling in love with the beautiful soul I glimpsed in your eyes."

I crushed my lips down over hers and poured my love into the kiss. "I promise," I murmured against her mouth a few minutes later. "We're going to have our happily ever after, sugar."

Epilogue 1
THATCHER

6-ish months later

All the whispering I heard going on in the kitchen stopped the second I walked into the room. I was surprised to see my wife sitting at the island with my sister-in-law, Blair. Justice hadn't said anything about coming by, and I hadn't seen Blair's shadow—her personal bodyguard, Benjamin—anywhere.

Kyla, Imogene's bodyguard, was standing just outside the back door, keeping an eye on the perimeter. Justice and I didn't fuck around when it came to our women. Being billionaires put you in the spotlight, and we were determined to do whatever it took to protect our families.

"Blair," I greeted. She and Imogene smiled innocently, and I immediately knew I was going to be forced to make an impossible decision. "Justice know you're here?" Both women immediately frowned and glanced at each other guiltily. I sighed. Either I pissed off my wife by "tattling" as she put it, or I got my ass kicked by my brother for not letting him know his wife had slipped her security and was at my house. It wouldn't matter to him that our place was as well protected as his. If Justice didn't have his or Benjamin's eyes on Blair at all times, he went ballistic. And, it had only gotten worse since she got pregnant.

"That's a no, right?"

Blair flushed, and her eyes darted away. "Um…"

If he didn't know she was here… "You turned off your GPS?" I guessed incredulously.

Her blush deepened, and she shrugged. "Just for a little while."

Son of a bitch. If I didn't diffuse this situation fast, I'd be bailing my brother out of jail for beating the shit out of someone.

Since I wasn't any better when it came to my wife…I had to go with door number two. Imogene would forgive me once I'd eaten her pussy to a couple of orgasms.

"Don't even think about it, Thatcher Kendall," Imogene snapped. "If you tattle, you will not get out of it by distracting me with…you know."

Blair giggled, and Imogene blushed adorably, making me grin. My smile turned into a wicked smirk as I walked over to the back of her stool and rested my hands on her swollen belly. "I bet I will," I murmured, my hot breath bathing the shell of her ear. Then I kissed her neck, which was easily done with her hair up in a ponytail. She shivered, and I chuckled. It was already a sensitive spot for her, but Imogene's pregnancy hormones were out of control. She was horny pretty much all the time. Not that I minded. "And, I'll prove it to you." Imogene squirmed, probably remembering all the ways I use to prove my point when necessary.

A buzzing sound drew my attention, and I glanced at the stone countertop to see Blair's cell phone vibrating. Her finger hovered over it for a beat, her face awash with indecision. Then she took a deep breath and hit the ignore button. I could only imagine the shocked look on my face. It started to ring again, and she glanced guiltily at the screen but didn't answer. Then she looked at Imogene. "We have to hurry."

The next second, my own phone was ringing. I dug it out of my pocket, unsurprised to see Justice's name flashing on the screen.

"Please, Thatcher?" Imogene pleaded with wide, tear-filled eyes. Shit. Another hormonal side-effect of her pregnancy, but one I hated. "We're trying to plan his surprise birthday party and since he never lets Blair out of his sight—a family trait, apparently," she interjected dryly, "she had to slip away." Imogene's whiskey orbs pleaded with me, and I felt myself caving when my phone began to ring again.

"I'm sorry, sugar, but if I couldn't get ahold of you and didn't know where you were, I'd lose my fucking mind."

I stabbed the button to accept the call. "She's fine, bro," I said quickly. "Sitting in my kitchen with my wife, and my security is watching over them."

Justice was silent, but I could hear his heavy breathing on the other end of the phone. When he finally spoke, his voice was raspy. "Thank fuck." Then he growled, "Put her on the fucking phone, Thatcher."

I held the phone out towards Blair, and she stared at it like it was going to bite her. "You're only getting yourself into more trouble," Imogene sighed.

Blair's shoulders dropped, and she reluctantly grabbed the cell phone. "Justice—" she started.

Standing as close as we were, we easily heard his reply when he interrupted her. "Do you have any idea how fucking worried I've been, bunny?" She tried to speak, but he cut her off once again. "No, don't say anything. You've already earned yourself a spanking. You'll be lucky if I don't chain you to our fucking bed. Now give the phone back to Thatcher and get your pretty little ass home." Blair huffed, making it clear she was annoyed but mumbled an affirmative. She'd started to hand it over when Justice called to her. "Bunny?"

"Yes?"

"I love you." Justice's voice was soft and full of emotion. "I wouldn't survive without you." Blair's whole demeanor seemed to melt, and her eyes took on a slightly dreamy quality.

"I love you, too." Just then, the doorbell rang, and Blair rolled her eyes. "Really? Benjamin is here already?"

I chuckled but quickly stifled it when Imogene and Blair both turned deadly, accusing eyes on me. I grabbed the phone and assured my brother that I would make sure Blair was delivered directly to her bodyguard before letting her out of my sight, then hung up.

I smoothed out my amused expression just as a tall, olive-skinned Italian dressed in a black suit sauntered into the kitchen. He glared right back at Blair, and my laughter slipped out again. Imogene smacked my arm, which only made me laugh harder. Especially when I really thought about the fact that Blair had pulled one over on the guy who was former Italian Special Forces and could probably kill a man with his pinky.

Kyla entered the room from the back porch at that moment, and she stopped short when she spotted Benjamin. Her expression turned smug, and he scowled at her while biting, "Shut it."

Her eyes widened with fake innocence, and she put her hand on her chest as though to say; Who? Me? "I didn't say a word," she protested.

"You were not saying it very fucking loudly," he growled.

"I don't know what you're talking about," she retorted. Then she walked over to him and put out her hand. Benjamin sighed and reached into his pocket, pulling out his wallet and withdrawing a one-hundred-dollar bill and slapping it into Kyla's outstretched palm. "You could have given me a heads up," he grumbled.

"What fun would that have been?"

Their exchange didn't make any sense to me,

and I turned to ask Imogene about it. She was looking anywhere except at me. Her bright pink cheeks and fidgeting hands had my senses on high alert. A quick glance at Blair showed her in much the same condition.

"Kyla."

"Yeah, boss?"

I kept my stare trained on Imogene as I asked, "Why does B owe you?"

She chuckled, and Imogene's blush deepened, making my eyes narrow. I took ahold of her chin and forced her to meet my eyes.

"We had a bet going. If our protectee managed to give us the slip, we had to pay the other one hundred bucks. Since he lost Blair, but Imogene couldn't shake me, he lost."

Imogene groaned. "Kyla! Where's the loyalty?"

Before another word was said, I shouted, "Everyone out!"

Within seconds, the room cleared, leaving only me and my wife. "You want to explain what Kyla was talking about, sugar?"

"Well, it's just that—I mean we didn't mean to be gone very long—but we didn't want our shadows reporting our whereabouts because we wanted to pick up Justice's presents, and if you knew where we went it would ruin the surprise." She grimaced when she saw my deep frown and the fury that I'm sure was blazing in my eyes. "We could only evade B, though. Kyla caught up with me before I could get even half-way to the meat-packing district and—"

"What the fuck?" I barked.

Imogene's mouth slammed shut when she realized the blunder she'd just made.

I shut my eyes and squeezed the bridge of my nose with two fingers. "Do you have any idea what could have happened to you down there by yourself, sugar?" I croaked. All of the scenarios were playing out in front of my eyes, each one worse than the last and leaving me more and more worked up.

When I lifted my lids, my wife was staring at my throat, remorse clear in her frown. I cupped her face and leaned my forehead against hers. I wanted to say something sweet and soothing, but I didn't have it in me at the moment. So, I just scooped her into my arms and stalked to the stairs, taking them two at a time until I reached our bedroom.

I decided Justice was on to something with his threat. Carefully, I laid Imogene on the bed, then retrieved a duffle I'd stashed underneath it on a whim one day. I unzipped it and dug through until I found the black silk ties and then tossed the bag away.

Imogene's eyes were round as saucers when she spotted what was in my hand. They were churning with a little wariness but also curiosity and desire. "What are you doing?"

"I'm going to tie you to our bed until I'm sure I've convinced you never to put yourself at risk again," I informed her in a firm tone. Quickly, I stripped off both of our clothes, then I climbed onto the bed and leaned over to secure one of her wrists. "First," I told her as I worked, "I'm going to prove my point by eating your pussy until you forgive me for siding with my brother"—I moved to the other wrist—"then, I'm going to spank your pretty little ass for disobeying me and ducking your security. After that, you're going to open that sexy mouth and suck me off until I'm too sated to think about everything that could have happened to you."

Imogene whimpered and rubbed her legs together, making my hard cock tighten while pre-come beaded on the tip. I tested the restraints, making sure they were tight enough to keep her in place but loose enough that they wouldn't hurt her.

"Then, I'm going to fuck your big tits and spill my come all over them to remind us both that you're mine." I scooted down and pushed her legs apart, settling between them and taking a deep inhale of her cinnamon and sugar scent. "And, if you're a very good girl, I'll fuck your tight pussy until you're screaming my name."

I kept my word and fulfilled all of my promises, but I still wasn't ready to release her. So, I fed her some dinner, then made slow, sweet love to her before taking off the silk ties and cuddling her into my embrace.

"I love you, sugar. You and our family are everything to me."

Imogene sighed and snuggled even closer. "I love you too, Thatcher." We were silent for a bit, then she cleared her throat, and I glanced down to see a blush sprinkling across her nose and cheeks. "Um…"

"What's wrong, sugar?"

"Nothing—um—I was just wondering…"

I raised a brow and waited.

"What else do you have in that bag?" She looked so eager and self-conscious at the same time; I couldn't help throwing my head back as I belted out a deep laugh. My wife was so fucking adorable.

Life with her was never boring. It was sweet, like cinnamon and sugar.

Epilogue 2
IMOGENE

4 years later...

I paused mid-stride when I stepped into our bedroom and spotted the duffel bag on our bed. We didn't get the chance to use the toys Thatcher kept in it nearly as often as we wanted, but that was understandable since having kids tended to limit our alone time. And once we were outnumbered, we had to get even more creative. Not that we let having three children under the age of four—Thatcher loved knocking me up, and I loved letting him because I wanted a big family—stop us. Our need for each other had only grown over the years, and we took advantage of every opportunity we got to indulge ourselves. Like now, when all of our little angels decided to go down for the night within fifteen minutes of each other.

Thatcher padded out of our bathroom, wearing nothing except a pair of black boxer briefs. His hard on pressed against the cotton fabric, and the sight made my pussy clench in need. He caught the look in my eyes as I ogled his body, and his lips curved up in a satisfied smirk. "You ready to pay the price for torturing me today, sugar?"

"Torture?" I lowered my head and peeked up at him from beneath my lashes, trying my best to look innocent. "You're going to have to be more specific because I have no idea what you're talking about."

"Uh huh. Sure, you don't." He stalked over to me and lifted me right off my feet to toss me onto the bed.

"Thatcher!" I squealed when he started to tug my shirt over my head. He tossed the material onto the floor and went after my sleep shorts and pulled them down. Before I knew what was happening, he had me completely naked, flat on my back, and was encircling my wrists with the fur-lined handcuffs he'd bought for me about a year ago.

Rising up on his knees between my thighs, my gorgeous husband's gray eyes darkened to the color of a stormy sky as they devoured my naked flesh.

"Don't even try to deny it, sugar. We both know you did it on purpose. You got me all worked up this afternoon, knowing I couldn't do a damn thing about it."

Heck yeah, I had. Teasing him was one of my favorite pastimes, mostly because it usually resulted in a memorable night for me. "Is this the part where I'm supposed to say I'm sorry?"

"Not quite yet, my beautiful Imogene." He reached out and pulled the duffel bag closer, his hand dipping inside to pull something out of it. I craned my neck to catch a glimpse of what it was, my eyes widening when I saw the vibrator. "But I'm willing to bet that soon enough you'll be ready to beg for my forgiveness."

"And we both know you'll give it to me," I whispered sassily as I widened my legs.

"Of course I will," he agreed, his head dipping low so he could twirl his tongue around one of my puckered nipples. As his mouth moved to the other side, he rasped, "If you need or want something, I'll always be the one to give it to you."

"But what if I'm in the mood to be the giver?"

Thatcher lifted his head and stretched out to cover my whole body with his muscular frame. I loved when he did that because it made me feel so safe and secure. His shortly trimmed beard scraped against the sensitive skin of my neck as he whispered, "Never doubt, not even for a minute, that you give me everything I need."

"Just like you do for me." I raised my knees to cradle his hips against mine, lifting my hips up to nudge against his hard length since I couldn't reach for it with my hands. "But I had something a little more specific in mind for tonight."

Thatcher pressed his palms against the mattress on either side of my shoulders and pushed up until he hovered over my body. "Oh, really?"

I licked my lips and murmured, "Yes, I wanted to torture you a little more, but with your cock in my mouth this time."

"Lucky for you, seeing your pretty lips wrapped around me sounds fantastic." He crawled up my body, his knees replacing his hands on either side of my shoulders and his hard length nudging against my lips. "And lucky for me, I'm in control of how much you get to torture me since you can only move when I let you."

Flicking my tongue out, I licked the drop of pre-come that had leaked from his cock, making him groan. Then I sucked him into my mouth. I tried to take as much of his length into my mouth as I could, keeping my eyes on Thatcher as I moved my head up and down. I loved seeing him lose control, knowing that I was the only woman in the world who had that kind of power over him.

"Fuck, yeah. Your mouth feels so good," he groaned, his hips pumping forward.

When his length pulled out of me on the next thrust, I twirled my tongue around the tip and flicked it along the slit. Then I sucked hard as he drove back in, hollowing out my cheeks. I felt him jerk in my mouth right before Thatcher wrapped his hand around my chin to control my movements. "Slow down, sugar. Your mouth isn't where I want to come, but I'm not ready to stop yet."

His command only spurred me on more, until a buzzing sound distracted me. With my mouth full of his dick and my hands handcuffed to the headboard, I couldn't see what he was doing. But I didn't have to guess for long because a short moment later, he rubbed the vibrator against my clit. I was already turned on to the point that I was drenched, and it didn't take much for the vibration to send me over the edge. I cried out around his length, and he pulled out of me to move down my body.

He kept the vibrator humming against my clit as he nudged my entrance with his hard length. I moaned loudly as I lay helpless beneath him, already craving another release. "Please, Thatcher. Come inside of me. I need you."

"I'm yours, sugar. Always," he promised as he rocked his hips forward, bottoming out when his cock bumped against my cervix.

"I'm so close," I panted.

Dropping the vibrator onto the mattress, he gripped my hips in his strong hands and lifted me up to meet his next thrust. My walls clenched around him as he pounded into me, over and over again until I finally flew apart. He surged into me twice more before planting himself deep and filling my pussy with his come.

After we caught our breath again, Thatcher rolled onto his side and undid the cuffs. "As much as I hate the thought of hurting you"—he trailed his fingers over the barely visible red marks on my wrists—"I love the idea of leaving more proof that you belong to me on your body."

"Yeah, because this isn't enough to do the job." Tilting my head back, I grinned up at him as I wiggled my fingers to show off the giant diamond engagement ring he'd given me, along with the matching band.

"I don't think anything will ever be enough for me when it comes to you." His hand dropped down to my belly. "But maybe we should see if another baby will do the trick."

Spoiler alert: he got me pregnant again that

night, but it didn't dim his possessiveness at all. Thank goodness.

CURIOUS ABOUT JAMISON AND HAZEL? Their Love is live! Want a FREE copy of The Virgin's Guardian? Sign up for our newsletter!

Epilogue 3
THATCHER

"Good grief," Imogene moaned as she padded out of the bathroom, looking pale and exhausted.

She'd been sleeping so hard that morning, so I'd fed Lucy, our youngest daughter, from a bottle, allowing my wife to rest. Three babies in three years weren't easy, but Imogene somehow managed to make it look like it was. She lit up like the Fourth of July at the simple mention of one of our children. But looking at her now, I started to wonder if it was taking a bigger toll on her than I'd realized.

We hadn't planned to have our babies so close together, but it seemed like all of the pregnancy prevention methods out there had banded together to boycott us. Plus, I couldn't keep my hands off of my wife, nor did I have any intention of trying.

After we had Allison, we'd decided to wait a year before getting pregnant again, so we attempted to use condoms. I'm a big guy, and unfortunately, the prophylactic companies out there didn't plan for men like me. Most of them broke the second I pushed into her tight pussy, if not before. Everett came along barely a year later. Then we tried birth control. It might have been successful if Imogene hadn't contracted the flu. It hadn't occurred to us until the positive pregnancy test that she'd probably vomited up her pills. After that, we both wanted to make sure we had a break, so she went to the doctor for an IUD. I loved seeing her pregnant, but I also wanted her to be ready whenever we had another child.

Considering her exhausted state at the moment, I was glad we'd made that decision. Now I was worried about what else could be wrong with her. "Sugar?" I rushed over to her just as she collapsed onto our bed. "What's wrong?"

Imogene opened her whiskey-colored eyes and glared at me. "Your freaking huge cock, Thatcher!" she snapped. "That's what's wrong with me!"

I blinked a few times, surprised and not sure how to respond. Indignation won out. "You love my dick, sugar. You tell me repeatedly every time I'm inside you."

Imogene groaned and flopped over onto her belly. "I'm going to sue my doctor," she grumbled with her face buried in the comforter.

"Imogene," I growled. "If you don't start explaining right this minute, I'm going to take you to the emergency room."

She sat up and opened her mouth to say something but froze before any words came out. Then she slapped a hand over her mouth and scrambled off of the bed before darting back to the bathroom. I rushed after her and grimaced when I heard the sounds of her getting sick.

"Do you have the flu again?" I softly asked as I dampened a washcloth and sat down beside her.

"No," she groaned as I gently wiped her face. "Four kids in four years...I'm going to lose my ever-loving mind."

"Four kids in—what?" I was confused for a minute until she speared me with a look that seemed to say, "Duh, Thatcher." Then it hit me. "Four?"

Imogene nodded and held up her hand, indicating that she needed help standing up. I scooped her into my arms before getting to my feet and setting her on the counter. "You're pregnant?" I clarified as I found her toothbrush and squirted on some toothpaste before handing it over.

"Yup. Your giant, birth control resistant cock has knocked me up, yet again."

I tried to hide my smile and the slight puffing of my chest—because the Neanderthal inside me was fucking proud of its accomplishment. Not to mention the flattering description of our dick. She narrowed her eyes, clearly not missing a thing.

She finished brushing and rinsed her mouth before giving me an adorable pout. "Seriously, Thatcher? Now is not the time to be smug."

I laughed and cupped her face in my palms. "I can't help it, sugar. You knew what a caveman I was when you married me."

Imogene sighed, but one corner of her mouth kicked up. "I did," she agreed.

"And you love me."

"I do."

I hesitated a moment, not sure if I should admit what I was feeling. Then I leaned in to place a soft kiss on her lips. "I can't say I'm sorry you're pregnant, sugar. We both want more kids, and honestly, even though you're so fucking sexy all the time, there is just something about seeing you knocked up…"

Imogene rolled her eyes. "It's that caveman again."

I shook my head and chuckled. "Maybe a little,

but I think it has more to do with your voracious appetite for my body when you're pregnant." I winked with a sly grin, making her laugh.

My hands drifted down until I was cupping her full tits in my hands. "I can't complain over the size of your tits, either."

Imogene moaned and leaned into my hands, her eyes drifting shut and a pink blush blooming on her cheeks. "They haven't gotten any smaller since my first pregnancy, Thatcher," she breathed. Her attempt to sound scolding failed when my thumbs brushed over her distended nipples and she sucked in a fast breath. "You—um—oh, damn, that feels good—but—um—I was saying"—I pinched the hard peaks before massaging the tender globes again, and she whimpered while squirming around on the countertop—"I'm trying to talk, Thatcher," she snapped before moaning and widening her legs so I could move to stand between them. Twin wet spots had appeared in the fabric of her shirt as milk leaked from her buds, and I licked my lips in anticipation of tasting it.

"Do you want me to stop?" I murmured while I leaned in to kiss the sensitive spot on her neck.

"No, dammit. I was just trying to say that my boobs are still big because you keep knocking me up before I'm done nursing!" She shouted the last of her words, then froze as her eyes frantically darted to the door.

I grinned and dropped my hands to the hem of her T-shirt—well, my T-shirt— and slowly began to draw it up her body. "Justice and Blair came and picked up the kids an hour ago." Before she could respond, I whipped the shirt over her head and resumed cupping her large, creamy globes. "Now, I want to get back to your point about feeding our babies."

"Wh-what?" she stuttered, her thoughts obviously scattering when I bent low to lick the white droplets off of her pink nipples.

"I'll always be addicted to your tits, sugar. But as you so eloquently pointed out,"—Imogene snorted making me smile as I brushed my nose over a sensitive tip—"I've definitely enjoyed having them fat and swollen, especially when they're filled with such delicious nectar." My lips wrapped around one glistening peak, and I sucked hard while my hands glided down to grasp her hips.

"Ooooooh," she moaned, thrusting her chest out, seeking more.

My cock was threatening to bust through my zipper. I let her nipple go with a pop and yanked her into my arms. Her legs automatically closed around me, and she tucked her head into the crook of my neck, latching on to the skin and pulling with gentle suction. I was losing control fast, and she knew it. "You're asking for it, sugar," I growled. She giggled, but it turned into a long moan when I grabbed her ass and pulled her center flush to the bulge in my pants.

Once I reached the bed, I spread her out on it and looked over her delectable body. Her lemon yellow panties were dark in the center from the growing wet spot. I licked my lips and tried to decide what to do first. After a moment, I practically ripped off my clothes then climbed onto the bed. I slowly drew down her underwear until it was all the way off and dropped them onto the floor. Then I shifted, so I was straddling her sexy, naked body.

One of her tits was red and swollen, having been well-loved by my mouth, so I got on all fours and lowered my head to give the neglected breast equal treatment. Her milk splashed into my mouth, and my dick leaked, dripping onto her already glistening pussy. After I'd had my fill, I released it and kissed each tip before taking Imogene's mouth in a deep, hungry kiss.

"I'll never get enough of you, sugar," I rasped against her lips.

"I love you, Thatcher."

Lifting my head, I stared into her beautiful, lust-fogged eyes and smiled tenderly. "I love you more than life, Imogene Kendall. To the moon and back." She beamed up at me and I cocked my head to the side, studying her. "Are you okay with this?"

Imogen smiled sweetly and rested her hands on her belly. "Of course, I am. I might be a little scared of having four children under the age of five, but I'll never be sorry to be carrying our baby."

I let out a relieved breath I hadn't realized I'd been holding. Part of me was confident of her answer, but a small worry that she was truly upset about being pregnant had lodged itself in my heart.

Imogene wrapped her legs around my hips and used them to put pressure on me so that my pelvis lowered just as she thrust up her hips. Suddenly, my cock was bathed in her warm, wet heat, and I groaned as I instinctively rubbed my dick through her folds. "Since I'm already pregnant, why don't we practice making more babies," she asked with a cute smirk.

"Anytime, sugar," I growled as I pulled back and lined myself up so that when I moved forward, my long, hard cock slowly pushed into her hot, tight channel.

"Oh, Oh! Thatcher!" She panted as she clenched around me, then whispered in my ear, "I need you, babe. Pretend you're filling my pussy with come so that you can prove to the world that I'm yours."

"Shit," I grunted. My wife knew exactly how to push me into losing control. "You want me to fuck you, sugar? Pound your pussy until it's raw and you feel me every time you move for a whole fucking week?"

"Yes! Oh, yes!" Imogen cried.

Far be it from me to deny my wife anything. So I gave myself over to instinct and threw her legs over one shoulder, closing them around my cock, making the fit even snugger. Then I planted my fists into the mattress and rested on my knees. I used the balls of my feet for extra leverage and began fucking my wife hard and deep, shoving my cock into her drenched pussy over and over like a prized stud rutting in a mare. "If you weren't already bred, you would be when I'm done with you, Imogene," I growled. "But since you are, I'm going to cream in you like I'm filling my favorite sugary pastry. Then I'm going to taste all that goodness while I eat your delicious little pussy until you come on my tongue."

"Thatcher! Yes! Yes!" Imogene always got hotter when I said dirty, filthy things while fucking her. It was one of my favorite things about her. My words caused her to cry out as her whole body clenched around me. It was actually painful, but the pleasure that came with it was more than worth it.

"Fuck! Fuck! Oh, fuck yeah, sugar!" I bellowed as I plowed inside, and her walls clamped around me, making it hard for me to retreat.

I quickly flipped one leg to my other shoulder and bent over her, pushing her wide open. Then I dropped my head and sucked one milky nipple into my mouth while I pummeled her pussy with eleven inches of hard, hot, steel.

"Yes! Yes!" Imogene screamed and her hands flew to my biceps, her nails digging deep into my flesh as her orgasm crashed over her. "Thatcher!!"

"Fuck, yes, baby. That's it, sugar, take me deep. Yes! Fuck! Your pussy is milking my cock just like your sexy little mouth when it's wrapped around me. Oh, fuck, yeah. I'm gonna come, baby. Fuck!"

My climax barreled through me so hard I roared with ecstasy as my vision blacked out. I continued to pump in and out until we'd both fallen over the edge again. Then I fell onto my back in a sweaty mess, breathing hard and trying to unscramble my brain.

"Holy crap, babe," Imogene panted.

I managed to muster up enough energy to turn my head and look at her with concern. "Shit! Are you alright? Did I hurt you?" I'd taken her harder than I'd intended, and I started kicking myself for forgetting to take it easy while she was pregnant.

Imogene sighed and rolled into my side, throwing my arm around her and tossing her leg over mine. "I'm perfect. That was amazing, Thatcher. Exhausting but so damn amazing."

"Are you sure?" I swiped away strands of hair that were sticking to her damp forehead.

Imogene giggled and nodded, her soft curls rubbing against my naked skin. "Since we didn't plan for the last three babies, you haven't made love to me intending to get me pregnant since Allison."

I grinned. "Maybe I have Justice's luck, and I just fucked one baby into two."

Imogen groaned and smacked me on the stomach. "Shut your mouth, Thatcher Kendall. I'm going to have my hands plenty full with four kids. Five would send me to Bellvue in a straight jacket." After a few minutes of silence, she popped up suddenly and stared at me with intense, narrowed eyes. "Considering our track record, if that's the way we're going to fuck after I have this baby, you're getting snipped."

Epilogue 4
IMOGENE

Coming up behind my gorgeous husband, I wrapped my arms around his waist and pressed my lips against his back. He turned around and claimed my mouth in a deep kiss, not the tiniest bit concerned that our kids were finishing up their breakfast directly behind us. Luckily, they were used to our public displays of affection and just kept on eating.

My bikini bottoms were more than a little damp by the time Thatcher lifted his head. "You taste even better than the delicious pancakes you made for breakfast."

I twined my arms around his neck and pulled his head down to whisper in his ear. "I can't wait until tonight when you can devour me like you did that big stack of pancakes you ate."

His gray eyes heated with desire as he pressed his hard on into my belly. "Maybe if we spend enough time down at the beach, Allison and Everett will go down for a nap with Lucy and Hayden this afternoon."

"It's worth a shot." I turned in his embrace to look through the floor to ceiling windows at our gorgeous view of the Atlantic Ocean. "I'm so glad you convinced me that we needed a house in the Hamptons. I love it here."

His hold on me tightened, and he dropped a kiss on the top of my head. "Me, too. You found the perfect place, sugar."

I snorted and rolled my eyes. "It wasn't too difficult for me to do when you told me to spend however much I wanted as long as I was happy with the house."

"The money didn't matter as much as getting the right place for all of us." He gave me a little squeeze. "Your happiness means everything to me."

"I know." I twisted my head around to smile up at him. Thatcher didn't just use his billions to make sure I had anything and everything I'd ever wanted. He also gave me the important stuff—his time, attention, and unwavering love. He was the best thing that had ever happened to me, and a day didn't go by that I wasn't grateful he'd fallen as hard for me as I had for him. "I love you."

"I love you, too."

My grin widened. "I know."

"You better." He wagged his brows. "But, I'm still going to thoroughly demonstrate how much I love you later."

Thinking about the box of toys we kept on the upper shelf of our walk-in closet, my bikini bottoms grew damper. "I'm looking forward to it."

"Alright, kiddos." Thatcher released me to stride over to the table and pull Hayden out of the high chair. "Who wants to head down to the beach?"

"Meeee!" Allison, Everett, and Lucy squealed in unison. Not wanting to be left out of the excitement, Hayden shrieked and clapped his hands.

"Allison and Everett, go change into your swimsuits," Thatcher instructed. Our two oldest children didn't hesitate to scamper off to their rooms. Cradling Hayden in one arm, he bent down to undo the strap on Lucy's booster seat. Then he took her hand to help her down. "I'll get these two ready if you'll clear the table. Leave the dishes in the sink, and I'll clean them up after we're done at the beach."

"You're seriously the best husband ever." I padded over to the table, pausing to kiss Thatcher's cheek before he headed out of the kitchen with our youngest kids.

By the time I finished cleaning up—including the dishes because I had plans later on for my man—he had all the kids ready to head down to the beach. Snagging the bag of towels and toys I kept in a big basket near the French doors leading out to the deck, I followed Thatcher and the kids outside. He carried Lucy and Hayden while I held onto Allison and Everett's hands to help them around the pool and down the stairs to the beach. Once everyone was situated in the sand with their favorite toys, I pulled off my cover-up.

"Fuck, it's a good thing this is a private beach." Thatcher traced his finger down my spine and dipped it into my bikini bottom. "You're too sexy in this for anyone else to see you. I'd be fighting guys off left and right to keep them away."

I giggled and pointed at our children. "You don't need to worry about other guys paying attention to me. Four kids are enough to scare anyone away."

He circled to stand in front of me and shook his head. "You seriously underestimate your sex appeal, sugar. How do you think you ended up with this many children so close together in the first place?"

"Because I love your dick so much," I mumbled

under my breath, my cheeks heating as I remembered how he'd used my favorite appendage last night after the kids fell asleep.

"Which is a damn good thing considering how much it likes to be inside you," he whispered as his hands glided to my butt to squeeze it. When his head jerked back and he bent low, I twisted around and glanced down to see what had surprised him but didn't see anything that would explain his reaction until he tugged my bikini bottoms lower and asked, "Where's your contraceptive patch?"

"My—" I yanked my bikini bottoms lower, making him growl even though there wasn't anyone nearby who could see my bare buttcheek. Not finding the patch where it was supposed to be, I stuck my hand inside to feel around for it and started to freak out when I didn't encounter anything. "Oh, crap! Where is it?"

"Crap, crap, crap," Everett chanted.

"Crap is a bad word. You aren't supposed to say it," Allison informed her brother, wagging her finger at him.

"But Mommy just said it," he argued.

"It's an adult word," Thatcher explained. "You can only say it when you're older."

Allison tilted her head to the side and asked, "How old?"

Everett put his hands on his hips and repeated, "Yeah, how old?"

If I'd been worried about anything other than birth control, my kids would've been cute enough to distract me from my predicament. But considering how often I'd been surprised by a pregnancy because the method we were using had failed, I couldn't let them divert my attention from the mystery of my missing contraceptive patch. While Thatcher lectured Allison and Everett about words they couldn't repeat, especially at school, I pulled my cell phone out of the beach bag and did a little research. What I found only freaked me out more. "Oh, crap."

"What is it?" Thatcher asked, peering over my shoulder to look at the screen.

I elbowed him in the side, twisting my neck to glare up at him. "It says that if the patch falls off for more than two days, then the chances are high that I'll get pregnant."

Thatcher's nose wrinkled as he thought for a moment and then said, "I hate to be the one to break it to you, but the last time I remember seeing the patch was more than two days ago."

"You and your huge cock struck again," I hissed, turning around and poking him in the chest.

His gaze dropped to my bare stomach, and he

shook his head. "Relax, sugar. You don't know that you're pregnant."

"It says right here that nine out of a hundred people get pregnant while using the patch!" I jabbed my finger at the screen of my phone. "I bet your super sperm knocked me up last night. Or the day before."

Reacting to my shrill tone, Hayden started to cry. I walked over and picked him up, and he snuggled into my chest. Thatcher rested his hand over our youngest's head and asked, "Would it really be so horrible to have another?"

I pressed a kiss to Hayden's forehead and looked at how happy the other three were to be playing in the sand. My eyes got a little misty as I answered, "Not even a little bit horrible."

It was a good thing I was okay with the possibility of being pregnant...because it turned out that I'd been right about his sperm. We had our fifth, and last, baby the following Spring.

Their Love

Billionaire Jamison Kennedy fell in love at first sight with his sweet, country girl. They were from different worlds, but he knew she was meant for him. He wasted no time in sweeping Hazel off her feet and tying the knot.

Hazel was desperately in love with her husband, but she didn't fit in with the glitz and glamor of New York high society. However, she was determined to be the perfect wife, even if it meant losing herself in the process.

. . .

Jamison knew something was wrong and he'd do anything to get back to the people they were when they first met. Because nothing was as important as their love.

Prologue
JAMISON

"One more," I growled as I shoved my tongue into my wife's tight channel. She cried out, and I licked my way up to her clit, sucking it hard as I filled her with my fingers. I'd lost count of the number of times I'd taken her over the two weeks since we'd been married, but each time, she was every bit as tight as when I popped her cherry on our wedding night. "Give me one more, peaches." I'd already wrung one orgasm out of her, but I was determined to get another. I wanted Hazel's cervix to be soft and her womb primed to take my seed when I finally sank my cock deep inside her.

In the next second, Hazel's hands dove into my hair and held on tight as she shouted my name while wave after wave of ecstasy crashed over her. I kept eating until the pulsing in her pussy began to dissipate, then I placed a soft kiss on her mound. I would never get enough of her taste; like peaches and cream.

She was panting, the movement bouncing her perky C-cups and making my mouth water to nibble on their hard, little tips. My hands dragged along her body as I moved up and over her. I was a few inches over six feet tall. At just barely five feet, she was tiny compared to me. My muscular body dwarfed her delicate one, and it made me feel even more protective, adding fuel to my already out of control obsession with my wife.

But, despite her slight frame, my girl was strong and could take everything I gave her in bed. I'd been afraid of hurting her at first, but on our wedding night, I'd lost myself to my mating instincts and ended up fucking her like a caveman. Afterwards, I'd mentally beat the shit out of myself for losing control and more than likely, scaring the crap out of my sweet, young wife. I'd done my best to hide the possessive, jealous beast raging inside me since we'd met. But when I finally claimed her, he refused to be contained any longer.

To my surprise, Hazel had clutched my ass, bucked her hips while kissing my neck, and asked, "Can we do that again?" Ever since then, she'd taken everything I had to give her; quickly losing her inhibitions and becoming a fucking tigress in bed.

Hazel gazed up at me with deep green eyes that were clouded with passion. "More," she whispered as she circled her legs around my waist.

"You want my cock, peaches?" I purred as I rubbed my thick shaft between her soaking wet folds.

"Yesss," she hissed as her muscles tightened.

I positioned my fat, swollen head at her entrance and circled my hips twice before I slammed my bare cock into her unprotected pussy.

We had two and a half more months before our honeymoon would be over, and I was determined to breed my little wife before reality intruded. Now that we were married, she was bound to discover just how deep my obsession with her went. I was fucking crazy over her, and I wasn't ever letting her go. She was finally wearing my ring, but I wanted her tied to me in every way possible.

Chapter 1
JAMISON

Hazel looked like a fucking goddess in a gold, strapless gown, with her hair curled on top of her head, and her features slightly enhanced by her subtle makeup. And it was pissing me the fuck off. If another asshole leered at her tits, I was going to ruin everything when I killed him.

My sweet girl was awed by the life we led, and I didn't want to burst Cinderella's bubble. She'd grown up in a small town in upstate New York. Her family owned an orchard, and I'd met her on my way to a meeting in Ithaca. I'd stopped by a roadside stand to buy some fruit, and she'd floated over to help me. She'd lifted her cherub face and smiled at me with her rosebud mouth, her green eyes twinkling, and the world had fallen away. I'd felt as though the ground had disappeared beneath my feet.

Like a fucking idiot, I'd simply stood there and stared at her. Her plump cheeks had turned pink, and she glanced down as she brushed long strands of coppery hair behind her shoulder.

She was young. Too young for me. She was wearing a pink headband with a checkered bow for fuck's sake.

"How old are you?" I asked. Then I silently berated myself, not only because those were the first damn words I'd ever spoken to her, but because my instantaneous, raging attraction had caused me to be rock hard and uncomfortable. Which meant the words came out a little too harsh.

She'd blushed harder and dug the toe of her pink canvas tennis shoe into the dirt. "Um, eighteen," she mumbled. "My birthday was yesterday."

I'd managed to stifle my huge sigh of relief. And yet…fucking eighteen? Damn, that made me seventeen years older than her. *Shit. Shit. Shit.*

"Happy birthday, peaches," I'd said in a much smoother tone. I wanted to reach out and run my finger over the pink dusting her cheeks and nose. I was betting that her skin was softer than silk.

"Peaches?" Her blush deepened, and her smile

widened, revealing two deep dimples. I was so fucked.

"I don't know your name, but you look like a peaches to me," I teased.

She'd giggled and flashed those lethal dimples my way again. "Hazel."

Beautiful.

When she beamed and thanked me, I realized I'd said it out loud.

"You're very handsome," she whispered shyly, making me want to preen like a damn peacock. I wasn't ignorant of my effect on women, I just hadn't cared before now. I wore my shortish, dark hair gelled into a style that was similar to a faux-hawk but acceptable in the business world. My green eyes were dark and fringed with thick, black lashes. My face was lean with a strong jaw and nose, covered with a neatly trimmed beard. According to some ridiculous articles and "sexiest whatever" lists, even the small scar on the top of my right cheekbone was appealing. Daily visits to the gym kept me cut and strong. I was lean but ripped as fuck. As her green eyes swept over me, I felt as though my skin had been singed by fire in every spot she looked.

I was about to reply when an older man who looked to be only a few years older than me had stepped behind her and watched me warily. From his features, it was easy to tell that he was her father. "Can I help you?" he'd asked gruffly.

My eyes had drifted down to my peaches again but lifted to her father's when he cleared his throat. I swallowed hard and forced myself to step away. I bought a few peaches—no other fruit appealed to me anymore—before dragging my ass back to my Maserati and lowering my big frame into the driver's seat.

I started the car and put it in drive, my eyes on her the whole time. My windows were tinted, but it seemed almost as though she could feel my gaze because she kept looking my way since her eyes met mine every time. It took everything in me to finally drive away. With every mile, it became clearer that I'd just made the biggest mistake of my life.

By the time I reached my destination, I'd realized what a huge fucking mistake I'd made. I called my secretary and had her make my apologies to my associates as I squealed tires and drove like a bat out of hell back to the fruit stand.

It took me a couple of days to convince her father to let me spend some time with her. If he'd pushed back even for one more day, I would have simply taken her. But it was clear that my girl loved her family, and I didn't want to cause a rift. Still, for those two days, I was never far from her. I couldn't stand it. I'd even found a back road onto their land and had spent a good portion of every night lurking near her window. Watching her sleep, knowing she was safe and peaceful, was the only thing that gave me any comfort.

When I was finally allowed to take her on a date, I'd pulled out all the stops, flying her back to NYC in a helicopter. I took her shopping for a dress, then we attended the ballet—since she had ballet slippers hanging in her room and ballerinas on her bedspread—and ended the night with dinner at The Rainbow Room. Throughout the night, she'd had a look of wonder on her sweet face as she chattered constantly. It was adorable and made me confident that my plan was working. I wanted to impress her, to sweep her off her feet and make her fall in love with me. If this was the life she wanted, I would give it to her. She could have anything she wanted, and I made sure she knew it. I also gave her light, teasing touches all night to get her used to me. From the shivers some of them elicited, I knew she felt the burn between us.

Her sweet innocence and genuine reactions had been refreshing and a huge turn on. But the more I'd gotten to know her, I found myself intrigued by her quick wit and intelligence. She was my little country bumpkin, and I hoped she'd never change.

When we returned to her town, I'd driven towards her home but pulled over a few miles from the house. Unable to stand it even another minute, I'd unbuckled her belt and dragged her onto my lap. A simple touch of our lips was all it took to have my body engulfed in flames. I wanted more—so much more—I wanted it all. But, not like that. I decided right then that our first time would be on our wedding night.

The next day, I had a talk with her parents. I told them I wanted their blessing but that either way, I was going to marry Hazel. I promised to take care of her, to love her, to give her everything her heart desired. Apparently, my passionate plea convinced them. Then her mother told me that our story wasn't so different from their own.

They called my girl into the room, and I got down on one knee to propose. Her whole face lit up, and she threw herself into my arms with a shout of "Jamison! Yes! Yes!" I laughed and stood, spinning her around.

I gave her a chaste kiss, mindful of the parental eyes watching us. Then I took the round, five-carat, peach sapphire on a rose gold band covered in tiny diamonds and slipped it on her delicate finger. Hazel had gasped, her face awash with shock. After a moment, her expression turned troubled.

"You don't like it?" I asked.

"It's lovely," she responded, her tone genuine. But it didn't erase the look on her face.

"You don't have to keep it, Hazel," I assured her. "You can have whatever you want. This just reminded me of you, peaches."

Hazel's expression had brightened, and she sent a soft look my way before shrugging sheepishly. "It's so big and expensive. What if I lose it?"

I couldn't help it; I threw my head back and laughed so hard that a tear leaked from the side of one eye. When I finally got ahold of myself, Hazel was watching me with an annoyed glint in her eye and her hands on her hips.

"I'm sorry, peaches. I guess we haven't really talked about it, but you are officially a billionaire, sweetheart. If you lose it, we'll just buy you another one."

Her jaw had dropped, and it was so adorable I had to sweep her up into my arms and kiss her until her father cleared his throat and tapped me on the shoulder.

"Save it for the wedding night, dear," her mother wisecracked.

Since that was the plan, I knew I needed to get my ass in gear and make the wedding happen. Fast. I called in every favor and used every ounce of my power to threaten, cajole, or blackmail people so I could give Hazel a Cinderella wedding in one month.

Unfortunately, some of the preparations needed to be handled in person, so I'd hired her a bodyguard immediately. However, even then, it had still been nearly impossible to go back to the city without her. I had a security system installed and had considered adding a camera to her bedroom, but I didn't want to risk her finding it and send her running before I got my wedding band on her finger.

I threw myself into the merger of my business and planning the most spectacular wedding since whichever royal got married recently and topped whichever one came before. The true miracle was securing St. Patrick's Old Cathedral for the ceremony. Luckily, I'd been a good Catholic boy growing up. And though I hadn't been back to church other than Christmas and Easter for years, I'd maintained a relationship with the priests. Plus, the marriage coordinator was my cousin. It also didn't hurt that I'd been a big donor already, and I promised to basically finance an entire major renovation in order to fast-track our wedding.

The reception had been at The Plaza, with the best of everything, and a guest list that rivaled the biggest A-list movie stars. I made sure my Hazel was the belle of the fucking ball.

I'd grown up in Queens, and all the glitz and glam wasn't really my scene, despite the billions in my bank account. But Hazel was worth it. She was worth everything.

Which was why I found myself at another stuffy charity ball, suffering through the sleazeballs that hid their depravity behind their money ogling my wife.

From the moment we'd left our Upper West Side townhouse, all I wanted to do was grab Hazel and run back inside and never leave. I hated sharing her, and after the news we'd received two days ago, I was feeling even more protective. You'd think knocking my wife up would ease the possessive bastard inside me. I mean, besides a ring, what else screamed "taken" better than a pregnant belly? However, it had done the opposite. I was more obsessed with my wife than ever, and every day it was a struggle to rein myself in.

"Jamie?" Hazel's soft, sweet voice floated up to my ears, making my cock swell. Generally, I fucking hated that nickname, but I loved the way she said it. Then again, I loved the way Hazel said or did anything.

"What do you need, peaches?" I asked with a

soft kiss on her temple. She sighed and leaned into me, and I tightened my arm around her waist. My eyes swept over her face, and I frowned at how pale she looked. Her green eyes had weary lines around them, and the sparkle that had drawn me to her from the beginning had dulled.

"I'm a little tired, would you mind if we went home?"

I was all too eager to comply with her request. "Of course, sweetheart." I began to guide her towards the coat check, but we were stopped at least three times along the way. They were all clients and despite my desire to bolt, I had to give them each a few minutes. I'd recently merged my business with K-Corp, another investment firm owned by brothers who happened to be two of my best friends. We all wanted to take a step back to spend more time with our families. Merging our companies, along with some smart hires, meant none of us were spending our entire lives in the office. Still, while it was an excellent business decision, it was a big one and some of my clients were still a little skittish.

Hazel greeted each of them with patience and a gracious smile. A frown tugged at my lips as I listened to her speak with them. Over the last month since we'd returned from our three-month honeymoon, Hazel's speech had begun to lose the country lilt and her tone was calm and refined, rather than high pitched and brimming with excitement. Less and less, I heard her cute farm girl phrases and the charming way she said, "y'all."

It confused me because I thought this was the life she wanted. To leave her small-town world behind and live in the fast lane. But it often felt like I was losing her. On more than one occasion, I'd been tempted to sweep her up and run away from the city and this high-society life. But, fear stopped me every time.

It took a lot of courage to accomplish everything I'd set out to do in my life. I was known for being fearless and going after the things I wanted. Just like with Hazel. I wouldn't have left that small little town until she was mine.

So, it was unsettling to find myself paralyzed by a single thought. What if Hazel wouldn't love me if I didn't come with this life? If it was just me and my overbearing, jealous, possessive ways.

Chapter 2
JAMISON

When we arrived home, I hung up our coats in the front hall closet while Hazel headed for the kitchen. I followed her through the arched doorway on my right and caught up to her just as she was standing on her tip-toes to reach the second shelf of one of the cabinets.

I walked up behind her and grasped her waist, lifting her off her feet and setting her on the counter. Then I easily plucked up the mug she'd been attempting to retrieve. In silence, I went about the task of making her some herbal tea. When it was finished, I filled her cup and waited for her to take a sip and hum in approval.

Son of a bitch. It was the same sound she made when her lips were wrapped around my dick. "Hold that carefully, peaches," I instructed before lifting her into my arms like a bride and carrying her up the first flight of stairs to our master suite.

I sat Hazel on the bed and took a step back, trying to calm the fuck down. I watched her as she sipped her tea and peeked up at me through her lashes with a slightly coy smile. It was appealing as fuck and made staying in control a mighty feat.

Ever since we confirmed that she was three months pregnant, I'd been extremely careful with her when we had sex. I missed fucking her, but making love with Hazel was also an out of this world experience. So, I focused on being gentle and loving.

Clenching my fists, I forced myself to turn away and take off my tux, then hang it in the closet; letting her have time to finish her tea and for me to get on steady ground.

"Jamie?"

"Yeah, peaches?" I popped my head out of the closet door to glance over at her. I suddenly felt like a fucking cartoon. My eyes bugged out, the dark green probably molten black from the lust coursing through me. My jaw dropped with my tongue lolling limply to the side, most likely dripping with drool. And my heart was pounding so loudly, I wondered if it was visibly banging out of my chest like a Bugs Bunny character.

Hazel had stripped out of her gown and was standing beside the bed in lingerie I hadn't known was hidden beneath it. Thank fuck, or I'd have killed every man who dared to look at her. Strike that, we never would have left the fucking bedroom.

She'd let her coppery hair fall in waves down her back, framing her gorgeous face. Her lush body was accentuated by the peach, lace teddy that barely contained her pregnancy swollen tits, caressed her slightly rounded tummy, and molded to the sweet curve of her hips as they flared. Garters and stockings made her legs look impossibly long for someone so petite, and she was still wearing the high, glittery-gold heels that had matched her dress.

Her eyes heated at my reaction, then they dropped to the substantial tent in my boxer briefs and a smug smile graced her pink lips. I swallowed hard and tried to stuff my tongue back in my suddenly dry mouth.

"Fuck me…" I croaked in audible thought.

"That's the plan, sexy," Hazel purred as she sauntered toward me.

When she stopped right in front of me, my hands darted out of their own volition and gripped her thickening waist. I lifted her, and she immediately wrapped her legs around me.

"You're so fucking gorgeous. What did I do to

deserve you?" Hazel's cheeks dusted with pink even as she beamed at me with pleasure. "You're my whole world, peaches. If anything ever happened to you, I'd be lost. I wouldn't survive."

She nodded and put one tiny hand on my cheek. "I know."

"It's why I do the things I do. To protect you." I placed my hand on her stomach. "There is nothing more precious to me than you and our baby." Again, she nodded, then brushed a sweet kiss against my lips.

I carried her as I padded across the plush carpet and set her on the bed. She reached for me, but I deftly caught her wrists and set them on either side of her head. "If you touch me, I won't be able to control myself."

Her green eyes burned with desire as she countered, "That sounds perfect to me. It isn't fair that I'm the one who gets to let loose while you have to hold back all the time. I want to drive you crazy sometimes, too."

It sounded fucking fantastic to me, as well. Keeping a tight rein on my rampaging libido wasn't easy. I'd love to sink my fat cock into her tight pussy and hammer away until neither of us could see straight, but I wasn't going to do anything to put her and our baby at risk. Their health and well-being took precedent over my raging desires—no matter how hard it was to hold myself back. The only thing that made it easier was knowing that I could still give her plenty of orgasms without having to worry about hurting her. Watching her as she flew apart and having her sweet taste fill my mouth had quickly become my favorite pastime.

"You'll never hear me complaining about you letting loose with me, peaches. I love to watch you come." Kissing down her chest, I swirled my tongue around one of her puckered nipples before adding, "But it's even better when I get to taste it, too."

"Yeah, but—"

Whatever she'd been about to say was cut off by a moan when I sucked her breast into my mouth and bit down gently on the tip. Being pregnant had made her tits sensitive as hell, to the point where I could almost make her come just by playing with them. With my control already near its breaking point, I used this to my advantage and focused on her breasts until she was writhing in need beneath me. Then I made my way down her body.

Gently resting one hand over her slightly rounded belly—as a reminder to myself about why I couldn't fuck her brains out—I glided the other down to spread her pussy lips apart. Then I lowered my head and licked up from her drenched hole to her clit. Humming in approval as the burst of sweet flavor hit my taste buds, I flattened my tongue and devoured her, licking from top to bottom and stiffening my tongue so I could thrust it inside her pussy on each downslide.

It didn't take long before her hips started to jerk up and she whimpered, "Please, Jamie. I'm so close."

"That's right, peaches. Give it to me," I murmured against her damp skin before I circled her clit with my thumb. Her entire body tensed before she cried out and her come filled my mouth. I licked her gently through her orgasm, waiting until her trembling stopped before crawling up her body and kicking off my boxers.

Before my cock could nudge against her soaked entrance, her small hand slid between our bodies to circle it. With her fingertips barely touching, I felt huge in her grasp. "I want a taste of you, too."

Even though my hips punched forward, pushing my hard length deeper into her palm, I wrapped my hand around her wrist and gently tugged until she let go of my dick. There wasn't a chance in hell I'd be able to maintain my control with her plump lips wrapped around my cock. The flare of disappointment in her beautiful green eyes killed me, but I'd never forgive myself if I let her push me over the edge and I ended up hurting her and the baby.

Determined to see her eyes full of passion instead, I claimed her lips in an ardent kiss and circled my hips with only an inch of my cock inside her pussy. "Some other time, peaches. I've been dying to sink into your wet heat all night. I can't wait another second."

"Okay," she answered softly, with a jerky nod. I could tell she wasn't thrilled by my refusal, but I knew I'd soon make her forget about it when I gave her another orgasm and let myself fill her with my come.

With that goal in mind, I slowly inched my way into her pussy until I bumped against her cervix. Then I pulled back and set a quick but careful pace as I thrust in and out of her, never going quite as deep as that first one. I kept one palm flat against the mattress, making sure I didn't give Hazel too much of my weight. Trailing kisses across her cheek, I brushed my lips over hers until she opened them. Our tongues tangled as our bodies moved in unison.

When I felt her pussy start to flutter around my dick, I grunted, "You feel so fucking perfect. Just like I knew you would with this sweet pussy milking my cock until I fill you up with my come."

"Oh—Yes—Please," she panted, her nails digging into my shoulders. I circled my hips, making sure to hit her G-spot on the next stroke, and she clamped down hard. With her cries of completion ringing in my ears, I finally gave in to the tingling in my spine. My cock jerked over and over again, and my hot come filled her to overflowing. With my chest heaving, I rolled off her body and collapsed against the mattress and pulled her on top of me. Her small hands stroked my chest, and she buried her face right above my thundering heart. It wasn't until she drifted off to sleep that I noticed a slight dampness on my skin. My lips curved up in a tiny grin at how fucking adorable she was, even when she was drooling on me.

Chapter 3
JAMISON

"I have to go into the office today, peaches," I murmured into her hair as I snuggled her close. "I want you to come with me."

She nodded and flipped around to cuddle into my chest, tucking her head under my chin. "Okay."

"How about I let you hang out with Blair at the daycare in the building instead of being stuck all day in my office?"

Her head dipped back, and her happy smile spread warmth through my chest and straight to my morning wood. "I'd like that."

Blair was the wife of Justice Kendall, one of my business partners, and she worked at the company daycare. I was actually a little jealous of his set up. He had eyes on his wife all day long because there were cameras everywhere. At the moment, I was forced to settle for a security team shadowing Hazel and GPS trackers in her ring and cell phone, on the rare occasions when I couldn't be with her. And, dragging her to my office to sit on my couch while I answered emails and had conference calls wasn't exactly fun for her. At least while she was in the daycare, I could watch her.

"Imogene will probably be there too, since the three of us are meeting today." Hazel's green eyes twinkled, and I almost groaned. I loved that she'd grown close with Blair and Thatcher Kendall's wife, Imogene. But it wasn't rare for the three of them to put their heads together and cause trouble. The kind that would put their husbands in an early grave.

Staring down at her delighted expression, I couldn't bring myself to care. I'd deal with that if it happened. At that moment, I was just happy to see her shine again.

I lowered my lips to hers, and it wasn't long before I had her on her back and was moving above her in slow, deep strokes. I deliberately kept a steady, controlled pace. I was determined not to lose my shit and turn into a fucking beast. I wouldn't risk being too rough and hurting her or the baby.

Hazel whimpered and moaned, "harder," but I

just shook my head and focused on giving her as much pleasure as possible.

"I love you more than anything, Hazel," I whispered, pushing her over the edge. She cried out, and the throbbing of her pussy had me following right behind. I pulled out immediately and started to roll to the side so I wouldn't crush her. She grabbed onto my torso and squeezed. "Don't go yet. I love to feel your weight on me." I was so tempted to give in to her plea, but I stayed firm and settled next to her on the bed. She sighed and muttered something so low that I only caught the word "breakable."

After a few minutes, her lashes lifted, and she stared up at me with eyes that were churning with emotion. "I love you," she whispered.

"I love you too, peaches," I replied with a smile before kissing the tip of her nose. She bit her lip as she continued to quietly study my face, almost as though she was searching for something. I wasn't sure whether she found it before she finally looked away. She cuddled into my side and traced her fingertips along the lines of my muscled chest.

Eventually, I dragged her cute little ass out of bed so we could shower together. I scrubbed her from head to toe, paying special attention to my favorite parts, including her slightly rounded belly.

When she was thoroughly cleaned and satisfied from two more orgasms, I quickly washed, then hopped out and grabbed a couple of towels. After wrapping Hazel up in the warm, fluffy material, I carried her into our massive walk-in closet. I dried us both and tossed the towels into a laundry bin. Then I rummaged through a couple of drawers in the dresser built into the center of the room until I found what I was looking for. After handing her the scraps of peach lace, I looked through her hanging clothes and selected a pretty, green sweater dress that matched her eyes.

Hazel watched me with amusement playing at the corners of her mouth. It was times like these, when I let myself get carried away in my obsession to control everything about her, that I worried she'd begin to see through my façade. So far, she'd either found my slips cute or hot. I definitely preferred when a show of my possession had her jumping my bones as soon as we were alone.

An hour later, I gave her a deep, passionate kiss before leaving her in the company of Blair and Imogene and heading up to my office on the forty-seventh floor.

Thatcher was already waiting for me, sprawled on one of the leather armchairs facing my desk. He was staring at his phone and barely acknowledged my presence. As I walked around him to sit at my desk, I glimpsed his screen and was unsurprised to see him glued to a video feed of his wife.

Since I pulled up the daycare security feed as soon as my computer booted up, I didn't comment. I started clearing through my emails until Justice joined us around ten minutes later.

Wordlessly, I swiveled my laptop to the side so that we all had at least a partial view of the split screen showing the feed from four different cameras. We'd never get any work done if we were all constantly checking our phones.

Justice grunted. "I don't like the way those three have their heads together," he muttered.

I was in complete agreement but had no solution, so I just shrugged. At that moment, Hazel threw back her head and laughed, bringing a smile to my face.

We jumped into company business for the next few hours; only stopping when it was time for lunch. "Let's take our girls out," Thatcher suggested, though from the look on his face, it was clear that he would rather grab his wife and hole up alone at home.

Once we'd collected our wives, I mentioned an upscale restaurant a few blocks away. Imogene's face wrinkled, and she pointed to a street vendor. "How about some hot dogs instead?"

Thatcher rolled his eyes and tugged his wife into his side. "No more street hot dogs, sugar. It's not good for you, but especially while you're pregnant."

Blair and Hazel screeched and started clapping and jumping up and down. They hugged Imogene who was blushing to the roots of her brown curls. "Our babies will be so close together!" gushed Blair. Hazel glanced at me with a question in her leafy green eyes. It was technically a little early, but I was as excited to share our news as she was. I smiled and gave her an encouraging nod.

Just then, Blair turned and grabbed my wife's hands. "Your turn, Hazel! Let's have our babies together!" Justice shook his head with an expression of exasperation, but he was chuckling.

"Perhaps we should let Jamison and Hazel decide when they want to have babies, bunny."

I couldn't help the huge grin that split my face when Hazel flushed and matched my expression.

"She's pregnant!" Imogene shrieked, and then the dance happened all over again.

We stood there a little awkwardly, but the proud puff of our chests didn't escape the girls' notice. Hazel smirked and cocked her head to the side. "Look at them," she jibed with a teasing tone that brought back the musical lilt from her country upbringing. "I'm surprised they don't float away with all those puffed chests and planet-sized egos."

I stuck my hands in my pockets and grinned unapologetically. Hell yeah, I was preening like a fucking peacock. My woman had a ring on her finger that could be seen from space and my baby in her belly. And right at that moment, she was glowing with happiness. I took a deep breath. For the first time in weeks, I felt easy and relaxed.

"IT'S ON WEDNESDAY. You guys are going to come, right?" Imogene was wringing her hands nervously as she voiced her question. It seemed she'd finally agreed to let Thatcher set up a showcase for her at a small, local gallery.

"Of course!" Hazel answered sweetly as she cuddled into my side. We'd ended up in a retro diner near the seaport where we could share a large, round booth, allowing each couple to sit together. She tipped her head back and looked up at me. "We can, right?"

"We can do whatever you want, peaches." She blushed prettily and gave me a beautiful smile. I fucking loved when she stared me like I hung the damn moon. I loved it a little too much because we were going to be stuck in that booth for a little while until I talked my cock down.

"It's casual," Imogene continued excitedly. "The gallery is actually kind of funky, so I think it will be a fun atmosphere."

The girls made more plans while we sat back and simply enjoyed watching them. I imagined my expression mirrored the one on Justice's and Thatcher's faces. Contentment and adoration. I was besotted with my gorgeous wife, and it reaffirmed my determination to do whatever it took to make her happy for the rest of our lives.

Chapter 4
JAMISON

Hazel had been practically beaming all night. I trailed behind her, keeping an eye out, but mostly just enjoying watching her. She was dressed in jeans that were a little too tight in my opinion, but hot as fuck. With a purple tunic that had long, flowy sleeves with slits in each one and another in the center of the chest, giving tantalizing glimpses of cleavage. She wore brown riding boots, and her hair was in a messy, fancy braid that hung over one shoulder, resting on her breast.

If she hadn't been so excited about attending the art show, I'd have kept her locked in the house while I devoured her from head to toe. It was still the plan for when we got home.

Imogene and Blair had drawn Hazel into a conversation about babies while I talked business with my partners. As time passed, more and more people arrived at the gallery, and I could tell that Justice and Thatcher were becoming as uncomfortable as I was. I sent a quick text and within five minutes, Bianca, Hazel's bodyguard, walked in the door. She was followed by Benjamin and Kyla, Blair and Imogene's security, respectively. When Hazel caught sight of the three "shadows" as the girls liked to call them, she rolled her eyes at me, but I just shrugged, not the least bit sorry.

They blended seamlessly into the crowd, and it allowed me to breathe a little easier. We'd all learned our lesson about security over the years since we'd made our first million, then billion. And, our wives were where we were the most vulnerable.

"Are you and Hazel attending the fundraising gala at The Met next weekend?" Justice asked, his eyes glued to his wife.

My eyes were similarly occupied, staring at my gorgeous wife. Every time she smiled or laughed, I felt my lips lift at the corner. Her joy was infectious. I responded to Justice with a nod. "It'll be another opportunity for me to unruffle some feathers with my clients. A lot of them will be in attendance, and I'm sure my Hazel will love it."

When the evening came to an end, the gallery informed Imogene that every single piece had sold.

The girls squealed and hugged in excitement, and warmth spread through my chest. I felt more at ease than I had in a while. Hazel seemed to be happy, and she was more like herself than she had been in a while.

"Did you have fun, peaches?" I asked her softly as she snuggled into my side in the back of our town car.

Hazel dropped her head back and grinned up at me, her green eyes dancing. "So much fun!" she exclaimed before leaning up to plant a kiss on my lips.

I slipped my index finger into the slit in her shirt right between her tits and ran the pad of my finger down the length of it. She shivered, and I grunted as my cock hardened painfully. "This has been driving me crazy all night. Did you do this on purpose, peaches?" I growled as I shifted her body until she was straddling my lap. She moaned when she felt my erection pressing up insistently between her legs.

"I think you intended to tease me." My hand fisted in the fabric and yanked, bringing her so close our lips were only a breath away. "Don't think I haven't been keeping a tally of all the spankings you're earning." I knew myself well enough to know that if I spanked her pretty little ass and saw my handprint on the white cheeks, I wouldn't be able to keep the devil inside me restrained. But as soon as she recovered from having the baby, it was going to be game on.

"Maybe you should punish me now," she breathed as she moved on top of me.

I gritted my teeth and set her back on the seat next to me. "You know I can't do that, Hazel." The happiness in her eyes dimmed, and I wanted to drop-kick my own ass for causing it. "Peaches, I can't lose control with you. I don't want to hurt you or the baby."

She blinked a few times, trying to hold back the moisture that was making it suddenly hard for me to breathe. "Are you sure that's all it is?" she asked in a tiny voice.

I took her chin between my thumb and forefinger, drawing her head up so I could look her in the face. "What do you mean?"

She tried to shake her head, but I was holding firm, so she swallowed and whispered, "Never mind. It's just pregnancy hormones messing with me."

The car came to a stop before I could dig further, and Hazel practically leapt from the car when Bianca opened the door.

I was tempted to rush after her, but something

told me that she needed some time. So, I headed for the kitchen and made her a cup of her favorite tea. Then I brought it with me to the bedroom.

Hazel was sitting at the vanity in our bathroom with the faucet in the big tub running. I set the tea in front of her, and she tossed me a small, but genuine, smile. I took over getting the bath ready for her, adding her favorite salts—ones I'd made sure she could use during her pregnancy—and setting a stack of warm, fluffy towels on a little table beside the bathtub. Then I grabbed the paperback from her nightstand. By then, the water was high enough to turn off the faucet. I helped her disrobe and step into the steaming water. She sighed and relaxed against the marble, allowing the water to cover her from neck to toe.

I stood and kissed the top of her head. "Call me if you need me, peaches."

It wasn't easy to leave Hazel alone in the bathroom—not when I wanted to climb in the tub and pull her onto my lap—but she looked like she needed to relax. I wasn't sure I'd be able to keep my hands off of her—and my dick out of her—If I had her wet and slippery, naked body pressed against me. My self-control had already been pushed to its limits. The last thing I needed to do was give it one final shove over the edge, especially when she seemed more vulnerable than usual. My job was to protect her, even from myself.

Padding into the walk-in, master closet, I stripped out of my clothes and grabbed one of my shirts and a pair of panties for Hazel to wear to bed. I set them on the edge of the mattress and turned down the sheets before heading downstairs to get my laptop. While I was there, I nabbed a snack and a couple of bottles of water to bring back up with me. I set everything down on the bedside table and noticed that there weren't any noises coming from the bathroom when I made it back upstairs. I nudged the door open, not wanting to startle Hazel if she was reading, and found her dozing off in the tub. Her tea and book were where I'd left them, so she must not have lasted long.

I carefully lifted her out of the water and wrapped her up in one of the towels. Her green eyes blinked open for a brief moment, and she sighed as they drifted shut again. My arms tightened around Hazel's curvy body when she cuddled against my chest, wrapping her arms around my neck. Moving over to the bed, I gently set her down and toweled her off. Once she was dry, I slipped my shirt over her head and tucked her under the sheets without bothering to slide her panties on.

It was going to be hell sleeping next to her all

night knowing that all I had to do was lift the soft material past her hips to get access to her pussy. But I wasn't about to risk waking her up while putting them on when she was exhausted enough to pass out in the tub. She needed the rest, and I was going to make sure she got it.

Pressing a light kiss against her forehead, I whispered, "Sleep well, peaches."

Chapter 5
JAMISON

"I can't believe I'm actually here, at the Met Gala of all places." Hazel's eyes were wide as she stared out the window of the limousine. She was so fucking gorgeous with her coppery hair piled on top of her head, a green dress that made her eyes pop even more than usual, and a King's ransom worth of diamonds and emeralds dripping from her ears, neck, and wrist. I'd surprised her with the jewelry right before we left for the party, and her eyes had gone round with shock when I'd put the earrings, necklace, and bracelet on her. She'd tried to argue that it was all too much, but I'd just kissed her until she blinked up at me with dazed eyes before helping her out of the house and into the car. "It's like we're in a movie or something, with all the famous people dressed to impress."

"None of them have anything on you." I trailed my fingertips along the neckline of her dress, over the swell of her tits. She looked down at my hand, and her breath caught. The sound reminded me of the moment right before she came, and my cock flexed against the zipper of my tuxedo pants. "You don't need the hair, make-up, or designer dress to stand out. You're already more beautiful than everyone else here."

Her gaze darted out the window again. "Right. Sure, I am."

The hint of sarcasm was impossible to miss and so unlike my sweet Hazel. It was difficult for me to wrap my head around the idea of my wife not knowing with every fiber of her being exactly how beautiful she was. The only thing I could figure was that maybe it was a pregnancy hormone thing, but I sure as fuck wasn't going to say that to her.

After a quick glance out the window to gauge how much time we had left before it was our turn to exit the limo, I slid off the seat and dropped to my knees in front of her. Taking her hands in mine, I squeezed them until she looked down at me. Keeping my eyes locked on her green orbs, I rumbled, "When I first spotted you at your parents' fruit stand, you were the prettiest thing I'd ever seen in my life. And you've only gotten more beautiful since then."

"Jamie," she sighed, shaking her head. "I just don't see how you can really think that. I've already gained fifteen pounds, and I'm not even halfway through my pregnancy. By the time I have our baby, I'm going to be as big as a...a...a hot air balloon!"

Her sputtering response and wide eyes were so fucking adorable—and more like the girl I'd fallen in love with—that I had to force my lips from curving up in a grin that I was certain she wouldn't appreciate in this moment. Lowering my head, I brought her left hand to her belly and placed it over the swell where our baby was growing. "Knowing that I popped your cherry and filled your womb with my baby is sexy as fuck. To me, every pound you gain is just more proof of how much you belong to me."

Her cheeks filled with a hint of pink as she rolled her eyes. "I guess it's a good thing you're looking at my baby weight that way because there's going to be lots and lots of proof for you to be proud of in the coming months."

I pressed a gentle kiss to her belly and wagged my brows. "You're not going to hear me complain. There'll just be more of you for me to love, and I fucking love the idea of that."

She shook her head and laughed lightly. "You're more than a little bit crazy. You know that, right?"

"Crazy for you, yeah," I agreed with a grin, immensely pleased to see her in a better mood.

My head jerked up when the driver called out, "Get ready, you're next up."

I nudged Hazel over and sat next to the door, so I'd be the first one out. Even though Bianca was in the front seat with the driver and would beat me to the curb, there was no way in hell anyone but me was going to help my wife out of the car.

After the limo rolled to a stop and one of the attendants opened the door, I climbed out and turned to offer my hand to Hazel. Her fingers trembled as she slid her palm against mine. I caught a glimpse of nerves in her gorgeous green eyes before she closed them and took a deep breath. When she stepped out and her feet hit the ground, it was as though all the ease I'd teased out of her disappeared. I didn't understand why it happened; all I knew was that I fucking hated to see her like this.

Wrapping my arm around her waist, I led Hazel down the carpet towards the steps and ignored any requests for us to pause for photos. She moved stiffly next to me, but that didn't stop most of the men from eating her figure up with their eyes when we entered the museum. She looked fucking gorgeous, but I hated how her dress emphasized the lusciousness of her tits and then flowed down in such a way that her baby bump wasn't visible. It made me want to beat my chest and roar out that she was mine. Since it was the wrong time and place for an over-the-top display, I appeased the beast inside me by tightening my hold on my wife as I guided her towards the table where Justice, Blair, Thatcher, and Imogene were already seated.

We were stopped a few times along the way by clients who wanted an introduction to my wife and to chat with me for a moment or two. Hazel mirrored the greeting the first of them gave us, flashing a smile that didn't shine nearly as bright as her usual as she echoed, "Hello, it's lovely to meet you."

She kept that smile plastered on her face as she listened to the conversation, nodding along with it every once in a while. Her reaction was much the same with the next couple, except the greeting she mimicked was "I'm delighted to make your acquaintance" that time. The third time around, she used both since the male client was by himself and was too busy gaping at my wife's tits to do much more than mutter a hello.

When we finally made it to our table, Hazel was still stilted even though there were only two other couples seated with us who she didn't know. It was obvious enough that Blair and Imogene sent her concerned looks, while Justice and Thatcher cocked their brows at me and jerked their chins in Hazel's direction as if to ask "What in the hell are you going to do about this?"

I didn't know what the fuck was going on with my wife, but I wanted my Hazel back. Not this version of her who was stiff and polite, like so many of the women who were a part of this glittery world. I wanted the girl who lit up my entire life with just one look.

Wrapping my hand around the back of her neck, I leaned to whisper in her ear, "What's wrong, peaches? Are you not feeling well?"

"I don't know what you mean. I'm perfectly fine." The smile she flashed me was brittle. It was also clearly not genuine since it didn't reach her pretty green eyes.

"You're not fine," I growled. "You're barely talking to your friends or me, and you look like you'd break if I touched you the wrong way."

Her gaze darted around, and her cheeks filled with heat. "I. Am. Fine," she insisted. "Please stop before people start wondering what we're arguing about. If we have to, we can talk about this later when we're alone."

Fuck worrying about what other people thought. Hazel's opinion was the only one who truly mattered to me. And fuck waiting for later. My wife was the most important person in my world. I wouldn't hesitate to burn my entire life down if that's what it took to make her happy.

Tossing my napkin on the table, I quickly rose from my chair. Gasps surrounded us when I lifted Hazel out of her chair and carried her through the room and out the door. I also heard the click of a ton of cameras. A picture of us as we left the gala was bound to make it into Page Six tomorrow, along with wild speculation about our marriage. But I didn't give a damn. The only thing I cared about was getting to the bottom of whatever was going on in my wife's head and fixing it so I could make her happy again.

Chapter 6
JAMISON

I barely resisted the urge to ravish her lusciously rounded body after I got her in the back of the car. She opened her mouth to say something, but my glare had her snapping her pretty lips shut. Her face was pink, clearly embarrassed by my display, but I couldn't muster up any regret. I'd had enough of this bullshit. I was going to get to the bottom of what was going on with my wife.

We rode in silence, but I claimed her hand and hauled her close so I could wrap an arm around her. She was still stiff, but our close proximity melted a little of her icy exterior.

Once we arrived at our home, I jumped out and gently pulled Hazel out behind me. Then I swept her into my arms again and took the steps to the front door two at a time. After punching in a code on the keypad beside the entrance, I pushed the door open and jogged up the stairs to our bedroom.

Stalking inside, I hit the light switch with my elbow, then set Hazel down in the center of the room.

She immediately spun around and punched her fists onto her hips. She was breathing hard, and I barely restrained myself from staring at her tits, keeping eye contact instead. It didn't stop my dick from responding, and it was on the verge of busting my zipper.

"Jamison!" she exclaimed hysterically. "Everyone is going to think you've lost your mind!"

Hearing my full name from her lips was the last straw. I swiftly closed the small gap between us and used both hands to grasp the scooped neckline of her satin gown. My adrenaline was at an all-time high, so it took little effort to rip the dress down the center. Hazel gasped, but I was too intent on getting her naked to determine whether it was from outrage or arousal. My tongue slid along my suddenly dry lips as I finally allowed my eyes to feast on her beautiful breasts while I pushed the green fabric off of her shoulders. My gaze followed the path of the dress as it fell and pooled on the ground. Her bra and panties matched her dress, and it pissed me the fuck off. Her entire outfit was a reminder of the aloof, socialite she'd become tonight.

I popped the front clasp on her bra and tugged it off of her. Then I tore away the tiny scrap of fabric standing between me and my wife's mouth-watering pussy. Finally, she was bare, and I used one hand on her back to press her body into mine. I was still fully clothed in my tux, but I could feel her heat penetrating through the layers, particularly where my cock bulged against her curved belly. My other hand slipped between us and just as I bent my head to capture her lips, I thrust two fingers into her soaking wet pussy.

Hazel sucked in a breath, and this time I was certain it was from desire. Her pelvis bucked and her tongue gave as good as it got, dancing furiously with mine. When she was panting with need, her body trembling with anticipation of her orgasm, I stilled my fingers and with monumental effort, tore my mouth from hers.

"Who owns this pussy, peaches?"

"You," she breathed immediately before her lips chased mine for another drugging kiss. I held back, not completely satisfied with her answer.

"Say my name, Hazel," I commanded.

"Jamison."

"Wrong fucking answer, peaches," I growled,

my grip on her tightening. Grasping her waist, I lifted her and laid her on her stomach in the center of our big bed.

"On all fours!" I snapped. She scrambled to obey, and it soothed me a little. But didn't lessen my fervor, my desperate need for her. I caressed one of her sweet cheeks and murmured, "Good girl."

I stripped off my clothes so fast it would have made Superman jealous, then climbed onto the bed behind her. "Say my name, baby," I crooned as I filled my hands with her round ass.

She glanced back at me in confusion and whispered, "Jamison."

Pulling my hand back, I brought it down on one lily-white cheek with a resounding slap. Hazel's eyes rolled into the back of her head, and she moaned. Mixing that with the bright red handprint marking her, I couldn't keep myself from coming just a little.

"You've earned yourself an ass so red you wouldn't be able to sit for a week," I growled. "But I'll settle for spanking you until you give me what I want." I smacked her ass and grunted, "with some extras for your behavior tonight."

Hazel's jaw dropped as she gaped at me over her shoulder. "My behavior? I did everything I could to be the perfect wife. To be sophisticated and elegant."

My eyes narrowed as I speared her with a dark glower. "Exactly." Smack. "I don't know what has come over you lately, but I want my wife back." Smack. "I don't want a plastic, cold, socialite." Smack. "I want the warm, funny, sweet woman I married."

"But—" Smack.

"Are you going to give her back to me?" I demanded, trying to keep the desperation out of my voice. Hazel turned her head forward for a moment, and I held my breath.

Then she looked back at me almost shyly, the adorable sight making my dick swell painfully. "I just wanted to be the perfect wife for you. To impress your clients and—"

I flatted one palm on the back of her neck before dragging it down her spine to the cute dimples above her ass. "You were already the perfect wife," I told her softly. "And for the record, you've always been worthy of being on my arm. If anyone wasn't worthy, it was me. I'll never be good enough for you, peaches. But I'm going to spend eternity trying."

Her expression softened, and she nodded as she gazed at me with love shining in her eyes. Relief trickled through my veins, but it was no match for the fire raging inside me. I wasn't going to be able to hold on much longer. "Now, give me what I want," I growled.

"Huh?" She looked confused, and I reiterated my command from earlier. "Say my name, peaches. I want to hear you admit out loud who owns every inch of this body."

"I did," she protested before repeating, "Jamison."

The crack of my next spanking rang off the walls. "Say my name, *peaches*." I grabbed my cock and squeezed, trying to stave off my orgasm. Then I slid the angry, purple head up and down the crack of her ass a couple times before slipping under and putting just the tip in then retreating.

"Jamie!" she shouted with a mixture of objection and naked want.

"Good girl," I purred. I slipped my hands around to cup her tits and played with her sensitive nipples while I placed wet, open-mouthed kisses on the back of her neck and down her back.

Hazel whined, and I spotted one of her hands inching toward her center. I grabbed it, then took hold of the other one as well. "Are you deliberately trying to provoke me, peaches?" I grunted. "You know the rule. Nobody plays with your delicious pussy but me." She glanced at me out of the corner of her eye, and I saw the sparkle in her beautiful green eyes that had been missing lately. The need to fuck her slammed into me so hard I almost collapsed on top of her. Inhaling slowly, I thought about investment statistics until I felt a measure of control return.

Wrapping her fingers around the spindles of our headboard, I leaned down to whisper in her ear. "Are you going to be good and leave your hands up here, or do I have to tie you to the bed?" Just the thought had come leaking incessantly from my cock.

"I'll be good."

Almost reluctantly, I released her hands and smoothed mine over her damp skin, once again palming the full globes of her tits. We'd get to bondage eventually, but tonight was about reconnecting, reminding her that I was the only one she ever needed to please and that meant being her true self.

I twisted and plucked at her fat nipples while my dick teased her pussy, sliding through her lips but never venturing inside.

"Jamie," she moaned, her ass wiggling, her body begging for more. "Please."

Hearing her nickname for me, said with such passion, fanned the flames licking at my skin. I needed to be inside her. I grabbed my cock and positioned it so that I could feed it to her inch by inch. I swallowed hard and silently reminded myself to be careful as I slowly penetrated her. She was so fucking tight it felt like she had a vice grip on me, but she was drenched so I still slid in with ease.

Hazel moaned and pushed back against me. I wrapped my hands around her hips and held her still as I fought to keep myself in check. Finally, I was balls deep inside her wet heat. *Fuck. Fuck. Fuck.* My spine tingled, and the need to pull back and thrust in hard and fast was almost overwhelming. My body and heart demanded that I prove who this woman belonged to. To fuck her with everything I had until she was marked inside and out. I was practically hyperventilating in my herculean effort to hold back.

"Jamie," Hazel whimpered desperately. "Please, please. I need you so bad."

Another notch in my determination slipped at her frantic plea before she added, "Fuck me, husband."

"Fuck!" I roared as the last thread to my self-control snapped. My hips shot back before plunging inside with enough force to bang the bed into the wall.

"Yessss!" Hazel screamed. She threw her head back, and I clenched a fist-full of her copper hair.

"That's it, baby," I growled. "Let go. Oh, fuck!" Her pussy contracted, and stars danced in front of my eyes from the acute pleasure. My hips pistoned in and out, hard and fast, bottoming out every time. Hazel's cries were quickly escalating to screams, and the world around me fell away. I was mindless, lost to the primal mating instinct consuming me.

"I want you bared to me, peaches," I managed to grit through clenched teeth. "I want you naked inside and out, don't hide anything from me." Suddenly, I realized that being in this position, I wouldn't be able to see her face when she came. It was one of my most favorite things because in that moment, Hazel was completely open, showing me her soul, giving me the gift of being completely vulnerable. Halting, I released her hair, then pried her fingers from the headboard. Quickly, I flipped onto my back and slid my head between her legs. I indulged in tasting her sweet pussy juices for a bit before guiding her body down so that she was straddling me. "Ride me, peaches." Her green eyes glowed, and she stared at me with the love and passion I knew she saw reflected in my gaze. I grasped her waist and slammed her down on my dick, then froze when I registered the thickness beneath my fingers. Hazel cried out and tried to move, but I held her in an iron grip. Terror ripped through me. I'd completely lost it and had fucked her with abandon. What if I'd hurt the baby?!

The next thing I knew, Hazel's small, warm hands were cupping my face, her lips only a breath away from mine. "You won't hurt us, Jamie." I shook my head and splayed my hands over the growing bump of her belly, but she nodded in a silent argument. Next, she brushed her lips tenderly over mine before sitting back, a stubborn expression on her face. "You asked me to give you all of me," she started, her tone firm but loving. "To be my true self with you."

I nodded warily, not sure where she was going with this. And, trying to ignore the way her pussy was gloving my aching cock at the moment, yelling at me to move.

"I'm more than willing to do it. But in return, you have to trust me."

"I do trust you," I immediately replied. It was the truth, I trusted her implicitly.

"Not if you don't believe me when I tell you that the baby and I will be just fine if you lose control with me. You won't hurt us, Jamie." Then she looked at me smugly. "The doctor even encouraged sex." I raised a brow. She'd called the doctor about this? It was a good thing her doctor was a woman, or I'd have been forced to beat the man until he forgot about anything involving my wife and sex. If the moment hadn't been so serious, I might have laughed at the absurd thought. Like I'd ever let her have a male doctor.

"Do you trust me?" she asked again.

I took a deep breath and groaned when it pushed my dick farther into her wet center. "Yes," I mumbled. I was distracted by the sensations shooting from my cock to my core, but I meant what I said. She seemed to know it because she smiled brightly and this time, it reached her eyes. My hands tightened around her for a moment, then I unclenched them and told her, "You set the pace, peaches. Take what you want."

Her green orbs darkened with hunger, and she began to move. Slowly at first, then increasing her speed until she was bouncing on my dick with wild abandon. Her full tits swayed in my face, the cherry tips hard and peaked. I sucked one into my mouth, and Hazel cried out as her walls closed around me so tight I worried for a beat that my cock might break off. "Fuck, Hazel," I grunted. "Your pussy is squeezing me so tight. You love my dick inside you, don't you?"

"Yes!" I wasn't sure if she was answering my question or responding to the sudden punch of my hips as I met her with an upward thrust.

"You want my come, baby?" I shifted to grip her ass, helping her to raise up and slam down on me so hard that the banging of the headboard joined our loud cries of passion and the sound of our slick bodies slapping together. "If you weren't already knocked up, I'd fill your womb so deeply and so full of my seed you'd be swelling with my baby in no time." I knifed up and pushed Hazel back, so she was lying on the bed. "I guess we'll just have to practice for the next one," I practically purred. She arched her back and moaned. "Does that make you hot, peaches? The thought of me putting another baby in you?" Hazel's head bobbed in affirmation, and it made the caveman inside me shout with approval. I spread her legs wide before gripping her ass once more. Then I got to my knees and lifted her pelvis so I could pump into her, hitting her cervix before rubbing along her g-spot as I dragged my cock back out.

"Oh! Yes! Jamie—I'm—I'm going to come!"

Quickly, I took hold of her arms and raised her so that she was once again straddling me. I pushed up from my knees and fucked into her tight channel every time she slammed down on my cock. The tingling in my spine was getting harder to ignore, and my balls were drawn up tight. "I love you, wife," I grunted.

"I love you, too," Hazel moaned as her eyes drifted shut.

"Come, peaches. But keep your eyes open, I want to see you when I make you explode."

Hazel dragged her lids up, and I locked our green eyes and poured out every bit of my love and obsession for her. Gliding my hands between us, I rubbed her swollen belly for a few seconds before using my thumb to rub her clit vigorously. She gasped and in the next second, she flew apart, shattering with an ear-piercing scream. I roared her name as I followed her right over the edge.

"I'M GOOD, Y'ALL," Hazel murmured into the phone as she glanced at me with a slight dusting of pink on her cheeks. "More than good." Her lips tipped up in a cat that ate the canary kind of smile. She sat on the bed, looking thoroughly fucked and satisfied as she talked to Blair and Imogen at the same time, who I gathered were sharing the phone on their end.

I grinned and crawled over my wife, settling between her legs that had instinctively widened for me. My hands traveled up her silky skin from her ankles to her thick thighs. Hazel's eyes rounded as she watched me, and I gave her a roguish smile before dipping my head to lick up the seam of her pussy. She stifled a sound and squirmed under my hold. "Um. Sure, I'll meet you—I—oh!" She shivered when I speared my tongue into her slick hole. At her exclamation, I gave her a dark frown.

"If you can't keep your sounds of passion quiet, I'll stop. Those are for my ears alone, peaches."

She nodded and pressed her lips together firmly. I rewarded her by blowing on her clit before sucking it into my mouth. "Yes!" she yelped. I stopped, and she begged me with her eyes to continue. "Yes, I'll see you at lunch tomorrow." I narrowed my eyes suspiciously, not completely convinced that she was simply agreeing to whatever the girls asked and not from my attention to her pussy. "I need to go!" she practically shouted before stabbing the screen and throwing her phone over the side of the bed.

I tsked and teased, "That was rude."

"Oh, for Pete's sake. It was your fault!" she snapped. "If you want to use that mouth, use it to make me come now that I've hung up on my friends so I can be as loud as you want."

Her words were like pouring a bucket of steaming water over me. I was suddenly on fire, my skin beading with sweat, and my cock springing a leak. It didn't matter that I'd fucked her brains out no more than a half hour ago; my cock was ready and willing to bring my peaches to as many screaming orgasms as she desired. "Yes, ma'am."

After two more rounds with my mouth and one on my dick, Hazel and I flopped back onto the bed, completely exhausted. I drew her into my arms, pulling her on top of me so her head was resting in the crook of my neck. "Do you remember what I asked you when we met?" I asked softly as my breathing returned to normal.

Hazel snorted. "I don't recall you asking for anything. However, I distinctly remember you demanding."

I slapped her ass lightly, and she squirmed at the sting. My face was buried in her hair, so I let myself smile. She was going to be a little sore tomorrow, and it gave me a smug sense of gratification.

"Okay," I responded after a minute. "Do you remember what I demanded?" I acquiesced.

"Besides marrying you?" she asked thoughtfully.

"Yes."

"You…" she trailed off for a minute then cleared her throat. "You asked me not to change."

I nodded, knowing she could feel the movement of my head. "To be very clear, I'll love you no matter what. And, change is inevitable, especially as you get older and mature. But, I'm just asking for you to keep true to yourself, peaches. Don't ever try to be what you think I want because I'll only ever want you, the real you."

Hazel sniffed, and I stiffened. "Fuck, peaches. I'm sorry. I didn't mean to upset you," I apologized quickly.

"I'm not upset," she insisted, but her voice was still watery, and I wasn't sure I believed her. Until she spoke again and soothed my worries. "That's the most beautiful thing anyone has ever said to me." Her head lifted, and she beamed at me, making her look like an angel. "I love you too, Jamie. Even your possessive, over-protective, obsessed sides." She giggled at her teasing, and it made me smile.

"Since I love you and you love me, I guess that makes us just perfect for each other," I quipped. Hazel giggled again and kissed my chest.

I turned onto my side and shifted her until we were in a spooning position, with her back to my front. Then I wrapped myself around her, cupping a tit in one hand and resting the other over her swollen belly. She drifted off as I drew light circles on her bump.

I couldn't wait to meet our little one. And I

couldn't wait to put another one in there just as soon as the doctor gave us the all-clear.

I loved seeing my woman pregnant, practically stamping her with "taken." It certainly didn't hurt that knocked up Hazel was insatiable. If I had my way, she was going to spend the foreseeable future with our babies growing inside her beautiful body. I hugged her a little closer and sighed with happiness before giving in to sleep.

Epilogue 1
JAMISON

1 year later...

"Just a minute!" Hazel yelled through the locked bathroom door. I knocked again, starting to get really worried. We'd been just about to start the christening ceremony for our daughter, Charlotte, or Charlie, when Hazel had turned green and bolted from the chapel.

"Peaches, if you don't open this door, I will knock it the fuck down!"

I heard a gasp from the other side of the door, then Hazel exclaimed, "You can't say fuck in church, Jamie! Do you want to burn in Hell?"

I stifled a laugh, especially since she'd failed to

realize she'd just uttered the same curse in the same damn church. But, if she heard me laughing, she'd cry, and I couldn't fucking stand her tears. Unfortunately, it was a common sight when my wife was knocked up.

"Baby, let me in. I just want to take care of you."

Hazel sniffled, and I sighed, mentally bracing myself to face her big, crocodile tears. They ripped me to shreds, but I tried not to show it. She'd just get more upset.

"Good grief! You got her pregnant again already?"

I turned at the exasperated question and saw Blair standing to my left. I shrugged, an unrepentant grin slicing across my face. As always, Justice wasn't far behind her and he grinned at me, giving me a fist bump and a slap on the back when he reached my side.

"Hazel, honey. It's Blair. Can I come in?"

I frowned and glared at Blair. "If anyone is going to go in there and take care of my wife, it's going to be me," I bit out.

A low growl rumbled from Justice, a subtle warning to watch how I spoke to his wife. I couldn't blame him since I would have done the same. I groaned and faced the door again. "Please, peaches," I begged.

The locked clicked a few beats later, and the door slowly pulled open. Hazel looked pale and so beautiful it almost made me weak in the knees.

"You're pregnant again?" Blair asked, her tone understanding.

Hazel nodded and shrugged sheepishly before pointing in my direction accusingly. "He wouldn't wear a freaking condom!"

I grinned, feeling not a single ounce of remorse. Yup, I'd totally knocked her up sometime in the week after the doctor gave us the green light. Hazel rolled her eyes, and her belligerent scowl matched the one on Blair's face. Except she was looking at her husband. Turned out, his expression matched mine and I couldn't keep it in this time, I burst out laughing.

Hazel's eyes darted between me, Blair, and Justice. She opened her mouth, hesitating before shutting it without saying anything. Then her eyes lit up as she suddenly realized why I was laughing.

"You, too?" she asked Blair excitedly.

Blair sighed and nodded, although anyone could tell from just one look that she wasn't really unhappy about being pregnant again. She was glowing, making me think of how Hazel looked when she wasn't suffering from morning sickness. That reminded me…

I pulled her into my arms and pushed her hair back from her face. "Are you alright?" She melted into me and smiled softly, her expression filled with love.

"Yeah. This baby just seems to dislike food a little more than Charlie did." She harrumphed and shook her head. "Not that Charlie has any problem eating now."

I bent my head and put my lips on her ear before whispering, "That's because you taste so fucking delicious." Hazel shivered, and my dick began to stiffen. "I haven't had my snack yet today, and I'm starving."

"Um, you two planning on having Charlie christened any time soon?" Imogene's voice broke through my lustful haze, and we all turned to see her walking toward us with our squirming little girl in her arms.

I gave Hazel a scorching look full of promise for later, and she licked her lips, her eyes darkening with hunger. Before I could give in to my desire to drag her back into that bathroom and suck her nipples dry and then fuck her up against the wall, I grabbed her hand and guided her back to the chapel.

The ceremony didn't last long, then all of our friends and family gathered back at our house for a reception. I just wanted everyone gone so I could get my wife naked, but she'd been looking forward to this day since Charlie was born. It had taken a little while to get it done because she wanted her parents to be there and they'd been unable to get away during the harvest season.

She looked so happy; I tried my best not to be a grumpy ass. Hazel had relaxed and fully returned to my cute little country bumpkin, and it made it impossible to say no to her. But I was going to need plenty of alone time with my wife later so she could make it up to me. I'd even put Hazel's parents up in a hotel and asked them to take Charlie for the night, which they were ecstatic to do.

Just then, Hazel glanced in my direction and seemed to read my dirty thoughts because her cheeks turned pink. I gave her an exaggerated wink, and she grinned in return.

It took another hour to clear out the last of the visitors, but then I finally had my wife all to myself. The time between the door closing and Hazel's first orgasm was however long it took to get rid of her dress, lift her up against the wall, and get my mouth on her pussy. She'd always been a quick trigger while pregnant, but she was even more hard up this time. I had a feeling it had to do with being pregnant and nursing at the same time.

After making her come with my mouth, twice, I quickly undid my pants as I got to my feet. Raising her up again, I guided her legs around my waist before thrusting in until I was completely sheathed. I groaned, the sound mingling with Hazel's moan. "Lose the bra," I growled. "It's time for Daddy's dessert."

Hazel hurried to undo the front clasp—something I insisted on for all of her bras—and her big tits spilled from their white lace confines. Her nipples were already beading with cream, and I latched onto one, drinking deep as I began to ram my fat cock into her tight pussy over and over.

"I fucking love these tits," I mumbled around a mouthful. "The only thing better than drinking from your sweet pussy is tasting your milky breasts."

I switched to her other nipple and licked up the liquid running down the side of her tit before sucking on the peak and drawing out even more of her nectar. Fuck, I would swear in court that her milk actually tasted like peaches.

Tearing my mouth away from her tits, I slammed it down on hers, letting her taste the remnants of her milk in my mouth. She moaned and attacked my lips with unbridled passion as her hips gyrated, meeting me thrust for thrust.

Without warning, Hazel's head flew back, and she screamed as an orgasm barreled through her. Her pussy clamped down so tight, I had no choice but to shout as I began shooting hot come into her womb; coming so hard I could barely manage to stay standing.

When it seemed like I was empty—for the moment at least—I rested my forehead on hers and concentrated on catching my breath. Hazel squirmed, and I grabbed her ass cheeks, stilling her movements. "I'm nowhere near done with you, peaches. But if you don't stop wiggling, I'm going to end up fucking you right here on the floor and I'd rather we be in our bed before I take you again."

Hazel sighed and leaned in close. She nipped my earlobe, making my only somewhat softened dick stand to attention once again. "Then hurry your cute ass up before I'm the one taking you to the ground and sucking your delicious cock until you can't see straight."

"Promises, promises," I joked, faking a grunt when she punched me in the arm.

Holding her close, I jogged up the stairs to our bedroom. I carefully lowered Hazel onto the bed and shucked my clothes before joining her. Then I pulled her into my arms and snuggled her close. Mindful of her pregnant state, I wanted to make sure she got some rest before the next round. And that's how the remainder of the night went; resting in between bouts of lovemaking and fucking. We also made very good use of the peach preserves her mother had brought from the orchard. It was early morning by the time Hazel finally gave in to exhaustion and fell into a deep sleep. As I held her, I thought about our family and drifted off with a smile on my face.

Epilogue 2
HAZEL

Two years later…

"Keep those eyes closed, peaches."

I pouted and crossed my arms over my chest. "Are we there yet?"

Jamison chuckled and patted my knee. "Patience, peaches. Patience."

"It's a surprise, mommy!" Charlie practically shouted from the backseat, and I heard her clap her hands.

The car turned slowly, and I heard what sounded like gravel crunching beneath the tires. Jamison had been up to something sneaky lately, and he brought Charlie into it as well. I couldn't believe I wasn't able to break her with cookies. He must have promised her something ridiculous for our three-year-old to keep a secret.

Our two-year-old, Lincoln, would have spilled the beans, but when I tried to bribe him, it became clear that he didn't know anything. Even seducing Jamison hadn't worked. Instead, he'd ended up talking me into waiting rather than me convincing him to tell me his little secret.

The vehicle finally rolled to a stop about thirty minutes after we'd left the city. "No peeing, mommy!" Lincoln shouted. I suppressed a giggle and exaggeratedly put my hands over my eyes.

"Okay, little man. No peeking."

I heard the car door open and shut, then I felt a soft breeze when mine was opened. Jamison took my hand and helped me out of the car. "Stay put, peaches."

From the sound of it, he was getting Charlie and Lincoln from the car. "Okay, guys," he said, "Let's show mommy her surprise." Two tiny hands took hold of each of mine, and the kids pulled me over to stand in another spot.

"Open your eyes!" they shouted. I lifted my lids and laughed at the sight of my children hopping around in front of me with excitement. Then I took a look at my surroundings. My brow furrowed in confusion as I stared at the big, restored plantation house, with a huge yard, situated in front of rows and rows of trees. It was a beautiful orchard.

"It's gorgeous," I breathed. "But it's too early to pick fruit from the trees."

Jamison chuckled and slipped his arms around my waist, splaying them over my slightly rounded tummy. "I guess we'll just have to stay here until they are."

Leaning my head back, I glanced up at him with raised eyebrows. "Stay here? Did you rent this place?"

His head bent, and he nuzzled my nose. "I bought it."

"We're home!" Charlie yelped, then she grabbed Lincoln's hand and they raced toward a play area on the left side of the house.

"What?" I didn't have any more words. I was confused, but hope bloomed in my chest.

"It's ours, peaches. We'll keep our house in the city, and I hired a couple to manage the orchard. But this is our home, where we'll raise our kids and grow old together." His expression turned nervous for a moment, and he asked, "Do you like it?"

"Like it?" I spun in his arms and threw my arms around his neck, hugging him with all my might. "I love it!"

He beamed at me before taking my lips in a deep kiss. "I love you, Hazel. There is nothing I wouldn't do for you, and I know this is the kind of place you dream about living."

I sucked in a breath and ducked my head while my cheeks bloomed pink. "Bianca's been pretty thorough in her reports to you, hasn't she?" I huffed.

Jamison laughed and buried his face in my neck. "No. I couldn't get anything out of that traitor." I giggled and silently thanked my bodyguard and friend. Jamison was an extremely hard guy to say no to. As was evidenced by the baby growing in my belly. I'd wanted to wait a little longer before we went for number three, but somewhere between two glasses of wine and several orgasms, I agreed to not using a condom—the one time! And look at me now…

"So?" I prompted. "How did you know?"

Jamison lifted his head and grinned, completely unapologetic about whatever he was about to say. "I hacked your Pinterest account, and I dug through the pages you follow on Facebook and found the one with old homes. You liked every single one that had land for an orchard."

I should probably have been mad at what he'd done, but the truth was, I was used to it. And, I'd learned over the years, everything Jamison did was to make his family safe and happy. Even when he was being an overprotective caveman, I couldn't help finding it incredibly sexy. He was an amazing husband and father.

"How about a tour of your new home?" Jamison whispered in my ear as he turned me around to face the structure. "After the kids go to sleep tonight, I'll introduce you thoroughly to our new bed."

I shivered with anticipation, and my panties became damp as my nipples puckered in response to his promise. He palmed my hips and pressed his hard cock into my ass. "Are you wet, peaches?" I nodded, and he growled. "I want to taste you so bad. I want to slip my hand between your thighs and plunge my fingers into your hot pussy. I want to spread your juices all over your hard nipples and suck them clean." I moaned and swayed as my knees weakened. Luckily, he had a firm grip on me and kept me upright. "Do you want my tongue or my cock first, baby?"

Before I could answer, the kids ran up to us and begged to go inside. Jamison held me in place, hiding the evidence of his arousal as he enthusiastically agreed. I giggled when he was forced to walk closely behind me. Although, our children were too engrossed in their new surroundings to pay us much attention.

They darted off as soon as we stepped inside. Suddenly, I was hauled back against my husband's hard, muscular body. He cupped my pussy over my jeans and pinched one of my nipples before palming my whole breast. "I don't know how I'm going to wait until tonight," he groaned, burying his face in my hair.

He twisted my nipple, and I shouted, "Nap time!"

NEXT UP IN the His Love series is Unexpected Love! Don't miss out on Fiona Davenport releases. Sign up for our Facebook group!

Epilogue 3
JAMISON

I stood on the back porch of our big plantation home and watched my wife dance around the orchard with our children. Their baskets of fruit were on the ground, long forgotten amid all their fun.

"Daddy! You're home!" London, our four-year-old daughter, shouted when she spotted me. "Come dance with us!" She ran over, holding out her hand, her expression making it clear that she fully expected me to obey her command. And since she had me wrapped around her little fingers, that's precisely what I did. She guided me over to Hazel, Charlotte, Lincoln, and Teagan, who were boogying to music coming from someone's cell phone.

When Hazel noticed me, she grinned and ran

over, throwing herself into my arms. I wrapped her in my embrace and lifted her off the ground so that I could plant a kiss on her rosy lips. When I pulled away, I grinned at the deep crimson staining her cheeks. "I missed you, peaches."

"I missed you too, Jamie," she said softly, love shining out of her beautiful eyes, warming me from the inside out like it always did.

I set her down and went down to my haunches with my arms open wide. All four of my babies crowded in for a group hug. I kissed the top of each head, earning me a groan from Lincoln and Teagan that made me chuckle.

I'd only been in the city for the day, and yet, I'd been bereft without my family. Damn, it felt good to be home. London wiggled from my arms and ran over to the cell phone, propped on a basket of ripe peaches. She turned it up and shouted, "I love this song!" She started hopping around in her version of dancing and singing about "funky toons."

I laughed as she grabbed my hand and tugged, watching me expectantly. Giving in, I danced around with her, and when everyone else joined in, I mentally chuckled at the sight we must have made. If Justice, Thatcher, and Jonah weren't as thoroughly whipped as I was, I could only imagine the endless amount of shit they would be heaping on me if they'd been here to see this. And I wouldn't care one fucking bit. Hazel had given me everything I'd ever dreamed of, and I wouldn't trade our life for anything.

Eventually, we all collapsed onto the ground, panting and laughing. Hazel was next to me, and she turned her head in my direction. She beamed at me, radiating happiness. "Welcome home."

———

"I FUCKING LOVE THESE BIG, sexy tits," I mumbled as I licked around Hazel's fat nipple. She moaned and arched her back, pressing herself further into my mouth and locked her legs around my waist.

My hips kept up their steady rhythm, pumping my long, aching cock into her virgin-tight pussy. Sometimes, I would swear she was even tighter now than the night I popped her cherry. Her walls spasmed, and her breath hitched, letting me know she was close.

"I'm gonna come, Jamie," she whimpered. Her voice sounded strained from fighting the desire to cry out. After expending so much energy earlier, the kids had passed out after dinner. I wasn't about to waste a second of our alone time and quickly hustled my wife to the bedroom.

I gently bit her nipple while my fingers twisted and plucked at the other one. "Let go, peaches," I commanded. "I want to feel your pussy milking my cock, squeezing the fuck out of me." I slithered a hand down to her soaked entrance and pinched her clit before slamming back in a little harder. Hazel buried her face in my neck to muffle her cry of ecstasy as she splintered apart.

Her pussy pulsed around my cock, and I quickly followed her into bliss. I lifted her face with one finger and crashed my mouth onto hers for a deep, passionate kiss. I made love to her mouth while I filled her with my essence, branding her as mine. No matter how many times I came inside her, I felt as though I was marking her for the first time. I was always desperate to make sure that the world knew she belonged to me and only me.

Finally, our racing hearts began to slow, and our breathing evened out. I pulled my wife into my arms and cuddled her close, placing a tender kiss on her temple. "I love you, peaches."

Hazel sighed and snuggled in a little more. "I never tire of hearing you say that." She kissed my chest and looked up at me with bright, shiny eyes. "I love you, too."

My skin burned where we touched, and her declaration, which never failed to get me hot, had my somewhat softened dick swelling into a steel rod. I smirked and gave her a wink. "How about we try and get in round two before—"

"Mommy! I'm thirsty!" Lincoln yelled through our bedroom door before knocking a few times.

"You were saying?" Hazel giggled. I glared at her, which only made her laugh even harder. She moved to get out of bed, but I stayed her with a hand on her arm.

"I'll take care of him, peaches. You rest up because as soon as my boy is asleep again, I'll be back for round two."

My voice was dark with promise as I climbed out of bed, and Hazel shivered, licking her lips as her eyes devoured my naked body. I worked hard to stay in shape, not only so I could keep up with my energetic wife and kids, but because it was worth it every time Hazel's eyes filled with lust when she looked at me. It also made it easier to keep the little shits who ignored her wedding ring from trying anything.

I grabbed a pair of sweats from the dresser and pulled them on before striding to our door and unlocking it. As I opened it, Lincoln stared up at me with eyes narrowed in accusation. "What took so long?" he asked with a dramatic stumble. "I'm parched. I could have died from dehydration. I hope you know."

I stifled my laugh and desire to roll my eyes and nodded solemnly, instead. "We can't have that. Who would help Teagan protect your mom and sisters when I'm gone?"

Lincoln's chest puffed up, and he turned to march toward the kitchen. "Exactly. What would you do without me?" His tone was smug, and since I was facing his back, I didn't bother to hide my grin.

"I'd be lost, little man," I told him honestly. Without my family, I would be lost.

Epilogue 4
HAZEL

"What did the boys do this time?" Jamie muttered after dropping into a seat across the desk from the elementary school's principal. We'd been called in to speak with Mrs. Simpson a few times over the five years since Lincoln had started kindergarten here, with Teagan only one year behind him. It'd never been anything major, mostly just boys being boys and they'd gotten off with a warning from the school.

Neither of the boys had gotten into trouble since Charlie had gone to middle school, though. They'd behaved themselves after Jamie had lectured them about setting a good example for their baby sister since her older sister wasn't in the same school anymore, and the boys took their responsibilities toward her very seriously. The call from Mrs.

Simpson this afternoon had been an unwelcome surprise, especially since it'd come while Jamie had been balls deep inside me. I'd just orgasmed the second time, but he hadn't finished yet. If it'd been anyone other than the school calling, we would have ignored it until he was done. But with our babies in their hands, we dropped whatever we were doing—even sex—and took any and all calls from the school. Even if my hubby was pissed our boys had gotten in trouble again...and beyond cranky because they'd managed to cock block him all the way from school.

"There was an incident on the playground during recess," Mrs. Simpson replied.

I twisted in my seat and glanced up at the clock on the wall, making my brows wrinkle in confusion because her answer didn't make any sense. "I don't understand. It's too early for the boys to be on the playground. They have recess after lunch."

Jamie's back straightened, and he gripped the chair arms so tightly that his knuckles turned white. "London just finished recess. Is she okay?"

"She was present during the incident, but she's fine," Mrs. Simpson assured us.

Jamie's shoulders slumped in relief, and I reached out for his hand. His palm slid against mine, and he gave me a comforting squeeze.

"As you pointed out, Lincoln and Teagan weren't supposed to be on the playground since it was the recess for first and second grades only. Apparently, they both asked for bathroom passes from their teachers at the same time and headed to the playground instead," she explained, lacing her fingers together as she rested her forearms on the table. "There was a boy—another first grader but in a different class than London. They went outside to team up against the boy."

"Lincoln and Teagan teamed up against a first-grade boy?" Jamie sounded as shocked as I felt.

"Um, yes." Her cheeks heated, and she cleared her throat. "It seems that the boy in question had pulled London's ponytail this morning when the first-grade classes were in the library. I'm not even sure how Lincoln and Teagan heard about it so quickly, but they said they went out there to protect their little sister from the boy."

"Some kid pulled London's hair?" Jamie growled, glaring at the principal. "And we're just now hearing about it?"

I let go of his hand to pat his thigh. "Before you fly off the handle, let her finish telling us what happened." I shifted my attention back to Mrs. Simpson. "I'm sure they handled it and brought the boy's parents in for a talk, too."

"Ah, no. Not yet. The boy didn't mean anything bad by it. He has a little crush on London and—"

"You can stop right there," Jamie interrupted, holding up his hand. "I don't care why he pulled London's ponytail. If some kid put his hand on my daughter, he'd better be punished for it. Especially considering the kind of stuff we've gotten called in for before."

I nodded, thinking about the time Lincoln pulled a prank on Teagan by putting a frowny face on his peanut butter and jelly sandwich when he helped me make their lunches—knowing his little brother only ate them one side at a time. Teagan refused to eat his lunch, and the teachers got involved. If something that minor resulted in us getting called to the principal's office, then some boy pulling London's hair should warrant a talk with his parents, too.

Well aware of how fierce we could be when protecting our children, Mrs. Simpson wisely agreed, "I'll call his parents as soon as we're done here."

"Good," Jamie bit out with a terse nod. "Now that we've settled that, how about you tell us what *exactly* our boys did to protect their sister that required us to come in for this meeting when the hair-pulling incident didn't even warrant a phone call informing us of what happened."

Uh-oh. I recognized that tone, and Jamie was pissed. Like blow his top, p-i-s-s-e-d pissed. I leaned back in my seat, knowing there wasn't anything I could do to stop the freight train that was my husband once his protective instincts were engaged.

"Like I said, the boys used their restroom passes to go out to the playground during first and second-grade recess. London pointed the boy out to them, and they cornered the boy to warn him away from their sister," she explained.

"They warned him away?" Jamie echoed softly.

Mrs. Simpson nodded. "Yes."

"How so?" he asked.

She tilted her head to the side. "Pardon?"

"How did my sons warn this boy away? With words? Or did they get physical?" he demanded.

"No, nothing like that." She shook her head. "They cornered the boy near the slide and told him that if he ever touched London again—with or without her permission—they'd make him wish he could transfer to another school."

"That's it?" He leaned back in his chair, crossing his arms over his chest.

"Um, y-yes," she stuttered, finally catching on to how angry Jamie was.

"So, let me get this straight." He crossed his legs and thrummed his fingers on his thigh. "Our sons didn't lay a finger on this boy, but we were called in here when he's the one who actually did touch our daughter. Is that correct?"

"Well, yes," she conceded. "Technically, he did touch London when he tugged on her ponytail."

"There's nothing technical about it." He stood and held a hand out for me. After I slid my palm against his, he helped me out of my seat. "We'll talk to the boys about misusing bathroom passes, and it won't happen in the future."

I barely held back my snort of laughter because I knew darn well he was going to tell Lincoln and Teagan that breaking the rules was okay if that's what it took to protect their sister. He'd probably get them a new video game as a reward, too. But she didn't need to know that...unless a situation like this came up again. And if it did, I had no doubt my boys would take care of it. They took after their daddy, after all.

DON'T MISS the next story in The Love Series, Unexpected Love! And if you're on Facebook, we'd love to have you join us in Fiona's Smutaholics!

About the Author

The writing duo of Elle Christensen and Rochelle Paige team up under the Fiona Davenport pen name to bring you sexy, insta-love stories filled with alpha males. If you want a quick & dirty read with a guaranteed happily ever after, then give Fiona Davenport a try!

Printed in Great Britain
by Amazon